Fine Spirits Served Here

Mary Walsh

ANNE
Do you believe
in ghosts?

Mary Walsh

Discover other titles by Mary Walsh

Copyright
Published by Mary Walsh
©2019 Mary Walsh

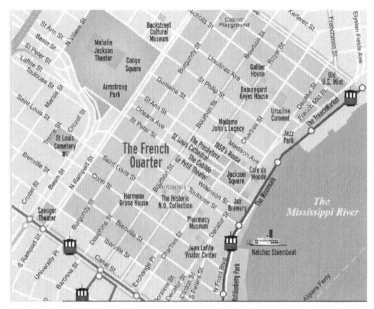

Map courtesy of ontheworldmap.com

This is a work of fiction intertwined with real establishments in New Orleans.

CHAPTER 1

"Who all here believes in ghosts?" the guide asked the small crowd of tourists on the sidewalk in front of Antoine's Restaurant on St. Louis Street. Antoine Alciatore opened the establishment in 1840 with its 14 unique dining rooms. Half a block away, late afternoon revelry from Bourbon Street musicians and sightseers faded into the French Quarter ambiance.

A few lax hands rose, almost reaching the strands of purple, green, and yellow plastic Mardi Gras beads hanging from a low hanging balcony. Newlyweds quietly giggled near the back of the group, more interested in each other than the tour guide. A retired couple stood front and center paying close attention. Harried parents with three rambunctious children in tow gathered in the middle. A few solo travelers filled out the rest. In the sweltering late August sun, no one wanted to wholeheartedly admit that they believed in the unknown. Hanging ferns on the second-story gallery gasped for breath in the sticky humidity.

"Well," she explained, wiping sweat off her brow, "legend has it that a ghost named Frédéric Boucher haunts Antoine's. He came here from France in 1863 searching for a new life and settled in New Orleans to earn his fortune. His true love Camille had planned to come the following year so they could get married, but her ship was lost at sea. Frédéric was so heartbroken when he learned the news of Camille's death, he went on a bender and drank himself to death. The next morning, one of the waiters on his way to work at Antoine's found Frédéric's body on this very street." The ever-happy tour guide motioned to the gray-squared cement beneath her feet. "It's possible we could be standing on the spot where the waiter found Frédéric dead of a broken heart."

The newlywed husband unsuccessfully stifled a snicker at the absurd thought. His wife snapped a picture of the oldest family-run restaurant in the nation.

The tour guide ignored the cynical man and pointed to the ironwork gallery on the second story. The retired man enthusiastically raised his phone to take a photo.

She continued, "These days, the staff inside Antoine's will say they've seen an apparition lurking at the windows on the second floor. They say it's Frédéric watching for Camille, still hoping she'll make it to New Orleans."

* * *

"Geez," I said to myself, peeking at the group through a sheer, white curtain inside the first floor of Antoine's. "Wait till those tourists check their pictures later. Then they'll see all sorts of orbs and spectral shapes hovering in the air. Don't they know the whole city is haunted? It's called the City of the Dead for a reason."

"Hey, Will," my buddy Terrance interrupted me, "let's go. Quit starin' out the window. The dinner crowd will be here in an hour. We need to prep." He headed toward the kitchen door.

"I'm comin'." I turned toward him and let the curtain drift back in place.

I had been working at Antoine's for many years, doing a little bit of everything. If the maître d' had to step away from the podium for a moment, I filled in. In the kitchen, I lent a hand washing dishes or putting the finishing touches on soups and salads. These days, I usually assisted in the dining rooms.

When Hurricane Katrina hit in August of 2005, I helped repair the damaged walls and collapsed floorboards. The four-story building buckled, the top two floors blew off during the megastorm, and the falling bricks crushed the adjacent building. After the storm, hundreds of pounds of decomposing lobsters, steaks, and soft-shell crabs in the walk-in freezer on the first floor needed to be shoveled out. Many long-time staff fled the area when their homes succumbed to the devastation. The entire 25,000 bottle rare-wine collection in the ground-level wine cellar was ruined when the power went off and the air conditioners died. We set up equipment on the street where the depleted returning kitchen staff cooked for first responders and construction workers. After months of repairing $16 million in damages and training new staff, we finally reopened that year right before the New Year's tourists invaded the Quarter.

Most of the staff at Antoine's have been here for years—some decades. One server named Sterling recently celebrated 50 years with us. He started his career when the menu was still in French and quickly learned how to translate it to his customers. In the past decade, his popularity meant that some of his regulars called him on his cell phone making sure he was scheduled to work when they wanted to come in to eat. Sterling told us about celebrities who dined with us over the years: Bob Hope, Tommy Lee Jones, Kevin Costner, Brad Pitt, and Nicolas Cage. Sterling loved recalling the story of when Whoopi Goldberg visited us. She made a point to meet all of the chefs in the kitchen and sign autographs.

I hustled over to Terrance. Like me, he wore the standard-issue black single-breasted suit, black bow tie, and white dress shirt. His ebony oxfords had been freshly polished. He kept his dark, curly hair clipped short into a fade. His name tag was perfectly attached to his left lapel. Terrance's deep brown skin matched the ceiling of the large annex dining room. He stood around six feet tall.

"While I check the tables, can you grab some towels and mop up the water in front of the kitchen door?" He pointed to a small pool of water on the wood floor in the high traffic area. "I think someone dropped a few ice cubes earlier. We don't need anyone slippin' and fallin'."

Terrance had started as an apprentice waiter when he was 22 and, after five years, was promoted to the youngest waiter on staff last year. He rode the streetcar to work and often worked double shifts. I recalled when his feet were killing him his first week, we took a quick break against the building on the corner of St. Louis and Royal Streets so he could rub out the knots in his soles. He questioned whether or not he made the right choice to work at Antoine's. I convinced him to stick it out and we became fast friends.

After grabbing some towels, I mopped up the water in front of the swinging kitchen doors.

"Did you know we have a new server startin' tomorrow?" Terrance adjusted the napkins on a four-top.

"No, I didn't," I replied.

"I hear she's worked in fine dinin' for many years and wants a change," Terrance said. "I think her name is Elle."

9

"L?" I questioned. "Like the letter?"

"No, dumbass," Terrance laughed. His pearly smile consumed his dark-skinned face. "Elle… E-L-L-E. Be nice to her. And don't scare her off."

"That only happened one time!" I took a step back and raised both hands in protest. "Geez, one offense, and I'm marked for life."

Two hours later, Terrance, the rest of the evening wait staff, and I scuttled around the large dining room. The dark red room quickly reached its capacity of 175 guests. Suspended from the ceiling, chandeliers with eight brass branches supported white glass globes with crystal stems dangling beneath. The crimson-colored walls boasted black-framed photos of city and state dignitaries, celebrities, presidents, and personal family portraits of the last seven generations of Alciatores who had owned Antoine's. White linen tablecloths covered every table and matching, starched white napkins folded into triangles rested atop them.

My whole body already ached from working for hours adjusting silverware, pushing doors open, and picking up dropped napkins. I scanned the dining room like a hawk searching for food, always anticipating our customers' needs. With a quiet moan, I remembered that, according to the maître d', the last reservation wasn't scheduled to arrive for another three hours.

The dinner crowd in curved wooden chairs represented a slice of life passing through the French Quarter. The dress code had relaxed over the years. Several older couples donned in prim dresses and linen suits were mixed among groups of 20-somethings sporting hoodies and tattooed arms. A man and a woman with a toddler tried to shush their little one when she attempted to have a conversation with another table.

A middle-aged man and woman huddled at a corner table of the dining room talking in hushed tones. They appeared to be on a date. A self-professed believer in romance, I dimmed the lights for them.

Terrance served a table of six our famous Baked Alaska for dessert. The football-shaped broiled meringue enclosed scrumptious layers of pound cake, vanilla ice cream, and chocolate syrup on a silver platter. "Happy Birthday Diane" was written in sugary, ivory meringue amongst white, billowy clouds of sweetness. Everyone at Diane's table oohed and ahhed at the specialty cake placed in front of them.

After Terrance left the birthday table, I caught sight of a small flame in the corner of my eye. Apparently, the pastry chef accidentally let the dessert torch singe the dessert a little too long and now a few embers slowly crept up the side of the cake. Not wanting to draw attention to an impending fire, I quickly skirted around the table and puffed the minuscule blaze out. Diane and her cohorts continued talking amongst themselves and didn't even notice.

Four hours later, the last table of three people in the dining room lingered over a bottle of 20-year-old Sandeman Imperial Tawny from our wine cellar. Not to rush them, Terrance anxiously waited for the sign of their nearly empty glasses to present their bill.

"When are these people goin' home? They've been here forever," I lamented, massaging a knot in my sore shoulder. Terrance and I loitered in the kitchen, occasionally peering out the window of the swinging door at the guests.

"If they get out of here pretty soon," Terrance said, "you wanna hit One Eyed Jacks?" After waiting tables with impossible guests all night, Terrance and I liked to get a break and be served ourselves. After hours, we often joined a few regulars up the block at One Eyed Jacks on Toulouse Street to catch some live music and burlesque shows. I usually hung back at the bar and people-watched while Terrance mingled with the lively groups of bachelorette parties.

"I don't think so, man," I replied. "I'm dead tired."

CHAPTER 2

My Darling,   21 July, 1863
    After seven weeks of traveling on a boat, I arrived in Vieux Carré a few days ago. Union Navy ships blocked the port, but my boat was allowed to pass through. I adore it here. I cannot wait to show you this beautiful city when you arrive next summer. Yesterday, I found a lovely house for us to live in on the far end of Rue Royale. My heart is so full thinking of you. You are my whole existence. I will love you until I take my last breath. I promise to send you a letter every week until I see your lovely face again.

Yours forever,
Frédéric

The next day, Terrance and I readied ourselves in the staff locker room while other servers and cooks wandered in to start their shifts. He shrugged into his black jacket, making sure it was straight.

"Did you end up at One Eyed Jacks last night?" I asked him, adjusting my bow tie.

"Yeah, it was cool," Terrance replied. "This one girl I met was super hot, man. We talked for a while, but when her friends came back to the bar, she went off with them, and I didn't see her again."

"Sounds like she ghosted you. Maybe she'll be back on Saturday?" I pondered, giving him wishful thinking.

"Maybe," Terrance said. "But you know me, I like havin' options. I could meet a different girl every night of the week if I wanted. One day I might settle down and get married, but that's not happenin' anytime soon."

"Oh, come on," I protested. "You said so yourself you don't want to be like that bartender Tony we met at Acme Oyster House the one night. I think he's pushin' 50 and has never been married. What does he have in his life except for millions of shucked oysters and empty glasses of Sazerac?"

"Maybe he'd rather share a bed with oysters and cocktails than women?" Terrance chuckled.

"Hey, you never know these days…" I said. "This city is full of weird people."

I followed Terrance out of the locker room and into the kitchen. Executive Chef Miguel held court as all of the wait staff gathered around him, pads and pens in hand. He wore a white chef's jacket with black trim and his name was stitched in black script across the right side of his chest. After beginning his career at Bienville House and Hotel Monteleone a few blocks away, Chef Miguel had been cooking for us for over 30 years. Despite the perception that most executive chefs had massive egos, Chef Miguel was unpretentious and treated all of us like family. And he knew how to cook. His decadent dishes earned the restaurant a Lifetime Achievement Award from the Louisiana Restaurant Association.

"Gather 'round everyone," Chef Miguel instructed. "Today's lunch specials include an appetizer choice of local charbroiled oysters, tomato basil soup, or a spring mix salad featurin' feta cheese, raspberries, and my balsamic dressin'." All of my coworkers hurriedly transcribed into their notebooks as Chef Miguel spoke.

He continued, "the lunch entree has three options as well. The fried drum fish is seasoned in salt, pepper, and cayenne, served with herb rice and spicy tomato piquant sauce. The drum was caught early this mornin', so

15

it's fresh. The second option is my personal favorite, a bowl of seafood and grits. The dish features shrimp and crawfish the size of a small child…" Chef Miguel chuckled at his joke, his eyes twinkling. "Okay, maybe not the size of a small child, but they're still big and covered in rich onion, tomato, and red wine sauce served over our buttery grits. The final lunch entree option is roasted French chicken breast with Yukon mashed potatoes drizzled with mushroom champagne sauce." He closed his eyes and moved his mouth in a slow chewing motion as if he was savoring each dish.

"What do we have for dessert today, Chef?" a server named Georgia piped up over the staff crowd, interrupting his daydream. She had been with us for ten years. Long enough to have enough seniority to request a Saturday off, but short enough that she could still keep up with those of us under the age of 30.

"Glad you asked," Chef Miguel replied, turning his head toward the stout woman. "We have a mixed berry compote of freshly picked strawberries and blackberries with a hint of lemon, mint, and rum, under a nice sized scoop of vanilla ice cream. The other dessert option is pecan bread puddin' full of golden raisins and pecans served with a praline rum sauce." He enunciated 'puh-KAWN' and 'PRAW-leen' in a velvety, southern accent reminiscent of native son Harry Connick, Jr.

"No PEE-cans and PRAY-leens for this crowd," I joked quietly to Terrance from the back of the crowd. If Chef Miguel knew how many discourteous Yankees in our dining rooms butchered the name of his favorite dessert, he might refuse to serve it to them and start another War of Northern Aggression.

"I have one more thing to announce before we get started," Chef Miguel declared. "I'd like to introduce y'all to our newest server, Elle."

A petite woman with mocha-colored skin and glossy dark hair twisted into the back of her head emerged from the crowd and stood next to Chef Miguel. She was in her early 30s. Her confident stature and soft facial features held my attention. She looked familiar to me, but I couldn't place her. I would have remembered someone with her uncommon name.

"Elle comes to us from Commander's Palace and, before that, K-Paul's," Chef Miguel told us, then motioned to her. "Elle, can you say a few words 'bout yourself?"

Ah, maybe I saw her at either of those restaurants?

"Thank you, Chef," Elle said, giving a quick nod to him. "I was born and raised in Bywater and now live a few blocks from my parents. I decided to work in the Quarter again so that I could be closer to home. I have five younger brothers and sisters and my parents gave me the reins of cookin' for everyone. I can't make Chateaubriand like Chef Miguel here, but I can make a mean jambalaya. I started waitin' tables when I was 18, and, despite the long hours that y'all know, I love it. I can't wait to work with all y'all." Despite being born and raised in New Orleans, Elle's voice had little southern accent except for her *y'alls* and dropping of her g's like the rest of us. I guessed she taught herself to speak more like a Yankee to be taken more seriously in the fine dining industry.

"Terrance," Chef Miguel called in our direction, "I'd like Elle to shadow you this week until she gets her bearin's. Teach her how we do things here. She is now one of the family."

"Sure thing, Chef," Terrance replied, giving me a knowing side-eye that he scored the attention of the cute new girl. He whispered to me, "She's a boss chick."

I smiled wide in agreement.

"And Will," Chef Miguel called to me, "since you know this place inside and out, give Elle a quick background on everythin' once lunch is over."

"You got it, Chef," I said, returning Terrance's side glance.

"Thanks, guys," Elle said to Terrance and me.

I knew I had met her before, but where?

During the lunch rush, Elle followed Terrance around the main dining room taking notes until she quickly learned to take orders without writing anything down. She occasionally stopped him to ask questions. She seemed eager to replicate our meticulous approach to fine dining.

Antoine's had set the standard for haute cuisine and crisp service in New Orleans for almost two centuries. The genteel restaurant wasn't highlighted in *Ten Restaurants that Changed America* by slacking off.

While Terrance took a quick bathroom break, Elle filled water glasses in the angelic, pristine room. Easing her way around tables, she was a natural in our dining room. As she squeezed her body between a four-top and an antique credenza, a man at the table suddenly scooted his chair back, forcing Elle to stop in her tracks and stumble backward. When Elle bumped into the large buffet table behind her, she caught herself and then headed toward the doorway. In the commotion, a tall glass vase of white roses on the credenza behind her bobbled back and forth. Thinking quickly, I rushed over and caught the vase of flowers before it crashed to the floor and settled it back on the countertop. Without noticing me, the man at the table didn't stop talking to his friends.

After the lunch crowd left, I brought Elle to the four private dining rooms on the second floor. We entered a large dining room that faced St. Louis Street. Floor-to-ceiling windows allowed the mid-afternoon sun to illuminate the room. Gold chandeliers with sparkling crowns suspended from the ceiling above us; scepters mounted to the walls around us.

"This is the Twelfth Night Revelers Suite," I told Elle. "This room was named after the Mardi Gras Carnival krewe that dates back to the mid-1800s. Their ball is held early in Carnival season and we host 20 to 30 events a year for them."

"Nice." She nodded with interest.

I led Elle toward the gold plaques on the far mossy green wall. "These brass tablets list every single queen of the krewe goin' back to the beginnin', except durin' the war years. Each year, all of the former queens come back to honor the new queen."

"You know enough about all of this that you could be a tour guide," Elle joked with a wink.

"Well, I *am* givin' you a tour." I laughed at my joke. "I've been here a long time. You get to know these things. This restaurant is a piece of the French Quarter. Everyone knows Antoine's."

"You know," Elle said, "I've lived in this city all my life and I learn somethin' new about it every day."

"Do you want to know somethin' else about this restaurant?" I asked her.

"Sure." Elle's blue eyes widened in wonder. Blue eyes on a dark-skinned woman were a rarity. I swear I had seen those eyes before. But where?

I leaned into her and whispered within inches of her ear, "It's haunted."

Elle barked a laugh. "Oh please! You can't be serious!"

20

I stepped back from her in response to her sudden laughter. "Dead serious," I said, settling myself a foot away. "A ghost haunts it."

"A ghost," Elle mocked me and flipped her hand in a waving motion in front of her. "Ooooh, scary."

"It's true," I said. "I swear."

"Oh, come on. I mean I've heard the stories about different buildings around the Quarter bein' haunted, like the LaLaurie Mansion down on Royal Street, but I've never seen proof of anythin'," she replied. "Those ghost tours make lots of money on gullible tourists, that's all."

"But this is true," I insisted. "Many of the staff here have seen the ghost of Frédéric Boucher. In the 1860s, he was madly in love with a French woman named Camille. She was supposed to come a year after he settled in the Quarter and they were goin' to get married. When he heard her ship sank, he drank himself to death on the street and has been seen lingerin' at these windows waitin' for her to come to him ever since. They say he couldn't go on without her."

Elle rolled her eyes at me. "Oh, please..."

"He's pretty harmless," I told her. "Our co-workers have described instances where they've seen Frédéric disappearin' into the walls or they feel a cold pocket of air even though they can't see him. Every now and then, he'll move dishes around in the restaurant or put fresh flowers into the vases overnight."

21

Elle arched an eyebrow at me, unconvinced.

"If you don't believe me, ask Terrance," I told her. "He'll back me up. He's even *talked* to the ghost."

"You expect me to believe that Terrance has spoken to a ghost?" Elle laughed. "And that he wasn't scared off?" She shook her head in disbelief. "You and Terrance can have your little séance parties, but I have better things to do." Elle took a few steps away from me, heading for the door.

"You are a skeptic, that's for sure. Maybe I'll convince you someday," I chuckled in defeat. I nodded toward the door leading to the hallway. "Let's check out the other rooms on this floor."

I gave Elle a tour of the large Japanese room, the Maison Verte room with two black marble fireplaces, and its twin, the Roy Alciatore room, named after the original owner's grandson who managed the restaurant through Prohibition and World War II. The wood paneling on the walls was taken from the old capitol building in Baton Rouge.

We made our way back downstairs and joined Terrance in the kitchen. He hunkered down at one of the tall metal tables eating from a white dessert plate.

"Chef Miguel had an overabundance of peaches this mornin' and made us Peach Melba for an afternoon snack," he said to us in between bites. With his fork, he motioned to the casserole dish full of the peaches along the wall to his left. "Get yourself a fork and plate and grab some."

"Thanks," Elle said. "I'd love to try it." She wandered off to get the sweet concoction of peaches, raspberry sauce, and toasted almonds.

"You're not goin' with her, Will?" Terrance gestured to me with his fork full of golden peaches.

"Nah, I'm good," I said.

"Did you learn anythin' about Elle when you took her upstairs and showed her around?" Terrance whispered to me. "I'm gonna ask her out. She's hot, man."

"Go for it," I chuckled, rubbing a hand along my chin. "The only thing I learned about Elle is that she doesn't believe in ghosts."

CHAPTER 3

My Darling,   *30 July, 1863*

Even though I do not know much about it, a war rages on around me. Yesterday, I attended a massive public funeral for a soldier named Andre Cailloux who was a former American slave. He joined the black American Union army and became a Captain. He was killed at the hands of the American Confederates and the city celebrated him with full military honours. Life is fragile, ma chérie. Please know that I would give my life for you like this man died for the freedom of his city.

  Yours forever,
  Frédéric

"What's wrong, man?" I asked Terrance after the lunch rush two days later. The long look on his face puzzled me. We lingered in the hallway of Antoine's, Terrance sipping a glass of ice water.

"She doesn't date coworkers," Terrance replied.

"Who doesn't date coworkers?" I nodded toward our cohorts heading toward the kitchen for lunch leftovers. "Oh, you mean Elle? You asked her out?"

"Yeah, I mean Elle," Terrance answered. "She turned me down last night after the dinner rush. Said somethin' about it bein' too complicated and went on about somethin' else, but, honestly, I have no idea what she said because I stopped listenin' once she said no."

"Well, you can always be friends with her," I offered.

Terrance snorted. "I'm not getting friend-zoned! She'll end up tellin' me about her shoppin' trips and visits to the nail salon and all I want to do is figure out how I'm goin' to--"

"Hey!" I interrupted. "Show some respect."

"I was goin' to say *kiss* her," Terrance replied. "Get your head out of the gutter."

"Well played, bro," I said with a nod. "Well played."

Terrance and I headed toward the kitchen and brought up the tail end of our coworkers in line for a late lunch. Chef Miguel dished out bowls of gumbo for everyone and laid them on the metal counter. Scents from the Creole Trinity gods of onion, green pepper, and celery filled the air. If heaven was a real place, it would be full of the provincial aromas.

* * *

An hour later, I wandered through the private dining rooms on the first floor, making sure chairs and tables were perfectly lined up for the next gathering.

"Will!" Elle called to me as I was about to enter the Proteus Room. A massive gold medallion on the wall depicted the Old Man of the Sea gripping a flaxen trident. "Somethin' weird just happened."

"What happened?" I asked her.

"I was in the wine cellar checkin' things out," Elle stated, her face a mix of annoyance and disbelief. "I turned on the light and walked in. Then I put my notepad down on a shelf as I checked out some bottles of port. The massive collection mesmerized me. I've never seen so many rare bottles. Anyway, I turned off the light and walked out. I got halfway down the hall and realized I

26

forgot my notepad. I went back in the cellar and the light was on."

I gazed into her aquamarine eyes, a slight I-told-you-so smile formed on my lips. Terrance may have had an issue only being friends with Elle, but I didn't.

"Don't even say it." Elle wagged a finger at me. "There are no such things as ghosts. Maybe someone else went in after me and I didn't see them, but I swear I turned the light off."

"It's okay to believe in ghosts, Elle. Really, it is," I assured her, almost grazing her arm. "Your secret is safe with me."

"But ghosts aren't real," Elle protested. "Maybe the light has a malfunction and the electricians need to come and fix it? Or maybe someone went in after me? Or... maybe I didn't turn it off when I thought I did?"

"After you've worked here a little while longer, you'll believe," I said.

"I doubt it," she replied.

I followed Elle back to the main dining room where Terrance waited for us near the servers' station with an empty water pitcher in his hand.

"What's wrong Elle?" he asked her, noticing the exasperated look on her face.

"Will tried to convince me that a ghost turned on the light in the wine cellar," she said.

"I believe it," Terrance replied. "That's what Frédéric does. He turns on lights, he moves glasses, he opens doors. But he's harmless."

"Don't tell me you buy into this whole haunted restaurant story too," she mocked him. "What a bunch of BS."

"Of course, I do," Terrance said. "Will and I have learned that if you are friendly to Frédéric, he won't do anythin' worthy of *The Exorcist* like shatter windows or send chills into the room or spin your head in circles. Everyone knows that around here and accepts it. I've even talked to him."

"Well yes, technically you can say somethin' to the ghost, but did the ghost talk *back* to you?" Elle countered, pushing her fists into her waist in protest. Until now, I had never noticed how short she was. She barely came up to Terrance's shoulders. She was a Doberman in the body of a Chihuahua.

"Yes, Frédéric talked back to me plenty of times," Terrance replied to the non-believer. "He speaks to everyone around here. Ask Chef Miguel. He'll tell you the same thing."

Elle scoffed in disbelief.

"Though this one time, Frédéric scared a customer when she wandered into the Tabasco room and he wasn't expectin' her," Terrance explained.

"Yeah, if I remember correctly," I interrupted, "utensils and glasses floatin' in the air. She screamed and ran off down the hall. Frédéric claimed it was a big misunderstandin', but the woman clearly saw everythin' and freaked out."

"How do most other customers feel about dinin' at a supposedly haunted restaurant?" Elle asked.

"They love it," I said. "Business is always boomin' because people want to catch a glimpse of a ghost. I think that's how the restaurant survived through Prohibition, World War II, and Katrina. And this is New Orleans. What buildin' *isn't* haunted? Anythin' is possible."

"Especially if you have enough booze," Elle added.

"You don't need alcohol to talk to Frédéric," I replied.

"Well, y'all can say what you want, but I still don't believe in ghosts." Elle rolled her eyes and bounded away.

Terrance and I hung back and chuckled at her skepticism.

"Well at least Elle isn't makin' it awkward that you asked her out," I said to him, as he filled the glass water pitcher in his hand.

"Yeah, really," he replied. "She seemed fine with me."

"Maybe the three of us can go over to One Eyed Jacks on Saturday and hang out?" I suggested.

"Good idea. But you ask her," Terrance replied. "Just so she knows that it's strictly a friends' night out. She might say no if I say somethin' to her, thinkin' that I'm still tryin' to get in her pants."

"Sure," I said. "No problem. I'll ask her later this week."

CHAPTER 4

My Darling,   3 August, 1863

Yesterday, after working at the port, I bought us a purple chaise, your favorite colour. I cannot wait for you to lay on it. I also commissioned an artist to paint a portrait of you from the photo in my billfold. It should be ready in a few months. I miss you so much, ma chérie.

Yours forever,
Frédéric

On Saturday, I approached Elle as we started our shift. "Hey, Elle, do you have plans after work tonight?"

"No." She arched an eyebrow at me. "Why?"

"Well, I was wonderin' if you would like to go over to One Eyed Jacks for a drink?" I asked her.

"Um, look, I appreciate the offer, but...." she said.

"Oh, no, no... it's not like that," I interrupted. "I'm not askin' you out. No offense, you're nice and all and you seem familiar to me, but I don't date coworkers either. What I meant to say is, do you want to go over with Terrance and me? We usually head there for drinks on Saturday nights after the dinner rush to unwind. Do you want to go with us?"

"And it's not a date?" Elle questioned. "And it's not y'all tryin' to get me into some weird threesome or anythin' like that?"

I chuckled. "No, it's not a date or anythin' weird." I raised my right palm to her. "I swear."

"In that case, then yes, I'll come with y'all," she replied, pushing a rogue strand of brown hair back behind her ear. "Sounds like fun."

"Good." I took two steps away from Elle. "I'll tell Terrance you're in."

"Wait." Elle reached toward me. "What did you mean when you said I'm familiar to you? Have we met before? I'm sorry if I don't remember."

I turned back to her, shifting my weight from one foot to another. "I don't know what it is, but I swear I've met you before."

"Have you been to K-Paul's or Commander's Palace? Maybe I was your server there?" she offered.

"I've been to both of those places, but I don't think that's how I know you," I sighed, curling the edge of my server's suit jacket in my fingers. "It's somethin' else, somethin' with your eyes, but I can't place it."

"My eyes?" Startled, Elle took a step back.

"Sorry, I'm not tryin' to be creepy," I reassured her, realizing I might have crossed a line. "I promise. But your eyes... I've seen them before. I know I have."

"Okay.... Well when you figure it out, let me know." Elle stared at me skeptically, but with a slightly upward turn of her mouth. "I'm pretty bad at rememberin' people. Ironic, since I'm a server, right?"

"How do you remember what customers order and correctly give it to the right person?" I asked. "I've seen you do it. You don't stand there like an idiot waitin' for the person to tell you what they got. God, I hate that when I go to other places that have sub-par service."

"At the other restaurants, I'd write myself little notes next to each person's order in my notepad," Elle explained. "Older man, chicken. Woman in pink, shrimp and grits. Young man in stripes, fish. For somethin' so simple to do, it gives impressive results. You'd think more servers would do it in other places. Even though we are taught as servers to start at the front of the table and go clockwise, it doesn't help when people change seats."

I nodded in agreement.

Elle continued, "But here we have to memorize everythin' without writin' anythin' down. That's been a little tough for me." She sheepishly grinned at me.

"You'll get the hang of it soon enough," I told her. "Terrance will help you."

"I hope so," she said.

"How do you like your first week anyway?" I asked.

"I love it," Elle said. "I was a little hesitant comin' in because I was afraid that everyone would be uptight and standoffish, but, so far, y'all have been patient with me bein' the new girl. It's like everyone is family here. And you and Terrance have made me feel especially welcome."

"Well, I'm glad to hear it," I replied. "Our stuffy black suits sometimes give off the wrong impression. We're tight here. That's why so many people stay for years. Sometimes decades."

"Well, I need to get back to work." Elle smiled at me. "Today is the last day I'm shadowin' Terrance, so I'll catch up with you after the dinner rush and we can head to the bar."

"Sounds like a plan," I said.

* * *

A half-hour after the last dinner guests finished their wine and paid their bill, I met up with Terrance and Elle on the sidewalk outside of Antoine's. If I didn't remember her short stature and captivating sky-blue eyes, I might not have recognized Elle. Now, her brown hair fell halfway down her back into thick curls, tightening from the oppressive humidity. She wore cut-off jean shorts and a plunging orange tank top that hugged her curvy body. Large silver earrings dropped from her ears. She was the opposite of her prim, genderless black and white work pantsuit and the requirement to pull her hair up at the restaurant. I quietly swooned when I discreetly eyed her up. Terrance did the same.

"I am ready for a drink!" Elle slapped her hands together. "We were so busy tonight. I barely had time to pee. I'll drink you boys under the table."

"Look who's talkin' smack her first week," Terrance exclaimed.

"She'll fit right in," I laughed.

"It takes a lot more than a cute smile to fit in around here," Terrance replied. "Let's bounce."

We took a left out of Antoine's and rounded the corner onto Royal Street. We passed Royal House Oyster Bar. Iron and glass lamps hung from the grey building, lighting our path. Like most other commercial buildings in the Quarter, the restaurant lacked first-floor windows;

instead, multiple tall open doorways promoted airflow in the thick humidity of the summer.

Passing snuggled candy-colored buildings of bright pink, sunshine yellow, and mint green, we dodged tourists window-shopping and gazing at the second-story wrought-iron galleries overflowing with flowers, strands of plastic beads, and colorful flags. Street musicians sitting on plastic crates played trumpets, saxophones, and guitars and serenaded onlookers nearby with tunes of blues, Americana, and southern funk. I loved this city.

In 1794, after a great fire destroyed most of the French Quarter for a second time, the Spanish overlords mandated strict new fire codes requiring all structures to be physically adjacent and close to the curb to create a firewall. As a result, the modern narrow sidewalks were barely wide enough for Terrance, Elle, and me to walk abreast.

Elle scoffed when we strode by a scruffy-looking woman sucking the last bit of a cigarette sitting at a folding table on the edge of the narrow street. Random-sized candles created a cheap-looking makeshift altar. A hand-drawn sign taped to the table offered to read palms for five dollars.

"What a joke," Elle quietly muttered to Terrance and me.

"I hear ya," Terrance replied. "I believe in the ghost at our restaurant but people like that only want to make a buck and will tell anyone what they want to hear. She's a quack."

We made the first right onto Toulouse Street. A red and black building in the middle of the block, One Eyed Jacks nestled unassumingly between a foot reflexologist and a custom frame shop. An abandoned bike was chained to one of the black poles that supported the second-story iron-lace gallery. Three bare lightbulbs illuminated the modest red and black round sign that hung from the underside of the gallery. A small crowd gathered on the front sidewalk anxiously waiting to be admitted by the bald, barrel-chested bouncer. The large man caught Terrance's eye and waved us in.

"You weren't jokin'. You really are regulars here," Elle laughed as we skirted the crowd.

"Yeah," I said. "When you've been comin' here as long as we have, Bald Rob lets you go right in. He should have checked your ID though."

"He can do it next time," Elle joked, as she used her diminutive size as an advantage to squeeze past people lingering in the entrance.

"You're comin' with us again?" Terrance pressed.

"Probably," Elle chuckled. "But the night's far from over."

Terrance and I laughed heartily, following Elle through the interior crowd.

Inside, Cajun music from the Lost Bayou Ramblers echoed throughout the venue whose color scheme matched the exterior. Terrance scurried ahead of Elle and led the way through the labyrinth of people toward the bar near the windows. A woman with cropped spiky blue hair, a silver ring in her lip, and a fleur-de-lis tattoo on her neck approached, the red lacquered bar separating us. A giant gold mirror behind her reflected the massive crowd of people in the place.

"What can I get for y'all?" she asked us.

Terrance offered his palm toward Elle in a "ladies first" gesture.

"Maker's Mark," Elle yelled to her above the loud music. "Neat."

The bartender beamed at Elle; her palms planted on top of the bar. "Damn girl." Then, she faced Terrance, with a hard glare that questioned his man-card. "And you?"

"The same," he shouted to her.

"Smart man," she replied. "Sixteen dollars. Do you want to start a tab?"

"Nah." Terrance pulled a twenty out of his wallet and slapped it on the bar in front of the mixologist. "Keep the change."

While the bartender stepped away to grab the whisky, Elle faced me.

"She didn't ask you what you wanted," she said.

"I don't drink," I told Elle, standing a foot away from her in the noisy and crowded bar.

"Seriously?" She raised an eyebrow. "You come here all the time and you don't drink?"

"Yup," I said. "But I used to. One night, I drank so much that I don't remember what happened. I swore to myself that I would never touch booze again."

"And you've stuck to it?" Elle asked. "In this town? Where everyone loves to party?" She motioned to the boisterous crowd encircling us.

"Yup."

Terrance interrupted us, handing a small glass of room-temperature amber liquid to Elle.

"Cheers," he said, clinking her glass with his.

"Thanks for askin' me to come out with y'all tonight," Elle said, swallowing the whisky in one gulp. She eyed Terrance's still-full glass. "Let's go. Drink up."

Terrance stuttered a few incoherent words at Elle's alcohol prowess as if he'd never seen a dainty girl down a shot before. He then followed her lead, slamming the empty glass on the counter in front of us.

"I told you she'd fit right in," I said.

Impressed, Elle said to Terrance, "Alright hotshot, can you handle a double? I'm buyin'."

"'Course. I'll drink whatever you're buyin'," Terrance boasted, cocking his head at her.

"Tough guy, eh? You don't scare me," Elle scoffed, mirroring his head cock. "You forget, I have five younger siblings that I had to keep in line. I've seen it all. I poured myself a couple of fingers of whisky every time I had to cover for them. Which happened a lot." She turned back toward the bartender and ordered two double shots of Maker's Mark.

After a couple more rounds of playfully one-upping each other, Elle slowly settled into a seat at a nearby empty barstool, steadying herself with her hand on the bar.

"You okay?" I asked, leaning into her. "You drink too much?"

"Yeah, I'm fine," she lied with glossy eyes. "Give me a minute."

"We can stop if you want," Terrance offered.

"Nah...." Elle said, trying hard to focus on something over my shoulder. Terrance and I both turned to determine what caught her attention.

Terrance and I rotated back, and I beamed at Elle. "I get it.... You think that guy back behind me is hot, don't you?" We all not-so-discreetly arched our necks back to get a better view of the man who stood tossing beers with some friends twenty feet away. His head of thick blonde hair and unblemished face stood out in a grunge sea of multicolor locks and facial piercings.

"Go talk to him," Terrance urged. "He won't bite."

"No, I can't, I can't," Elle protested, inching herself away from us, allowing the bar to give her security.

"You think some dude will blow you off if you go up and say hi?" I countered.

"Yeah," Elle replied.

"Oh, come on. We live for that stuff. If a hot girl came up to me, I'd be totally down with it," Terrance said. "I wish it would happen *more* often."

"I just ... can't," Elle stuttered.

"You talk to strangers all the time at work," I said. "How's this different?"

"It's different because she thinks this guy is hot and she's too embarrassed to talk to him," Terrance teased her.

"Go say hi to him," I pressed. "If you don't, I will."

Elle didn't budge.

I stepped away from Terrance and Elle and headed toward Elle's crush. Standing behind him, I pointed to him and yelled loudly, "You mean you think this guy is hot?"

"No!" Elle jumped up from her seat. "You're a dead man!"

Elle abandoned Terrance with a determined swagger. She nudged her way around a few people in her path, marched toward the blonde guy near me, and tapped him on the shoulder. He faced her and they started talking.

I hightailed it away from them and headed back to Terrance, leaving Elle to talk to her mystery man.

CHAPTER 5

My Darling,   12 August, 1863
    While I was at the port today, a commission merchant approached me and asked if I wanted to be his apprentice. He said I had a nice look. I agreed and I will start working for him tomorrow. Hopefully, this means I can save money faster and have a lovely home ready when you finally get here. I cannot wait to kiss your heavenly lips again.
    Yours forever,
    Frédéric

43

Terrance and I didn't work the Sunday Jazz Brunch, so it was nice to have a day-long reprieve until we met up again prepping for Monday's lunch crowd. I found him filling water carafes in the main dining room.

"What did you do on your day off?" I asked him.

"Not much," he said. "I had every intention of cleanin' my place for when my parents come visit, but this heat wave is a killer. I ended up watchin' the Saints preseason game."

"Yeah, the weatherman said it will be over 100 for the next two weeks," I added.

"Ugh, brutal," Terrance sighed.

"Did you talk to Elle after she ditched us on Saturday?" I asked.

"No, did you?"

"No," I said. "I'm dyin' to see what happened with that guy after she left us in a huff. You *know* she's gettin' me back for that."

"No doubt," Terrance chuckled. "Watch your back, bro."

I barked a laugh. "Okay, man, I'll catch ya later." I left Terrance and headed toward the kitchen.

Chef Miguel greeted me with his typical wide smile. "How are you doin' today, Will?"

"Good thanks," I said. "You?"

"Waitin' for some oysters to be delivered so that the kitchen staff and I can start preppin' Oysters Rockefeller. Seems the delivery man missed us this mornin'," he said. "But otherwise, it's a great day!"

Leave it up to Chef Miguel to turn filling oysters into something upbeat and fun. He held the secret recipe to the special green sauce under tight wraps.

Twenty minutes later, I wandered through the first-floor hallway, checking each private dining room for readiness.

The Mystery Room earned its moniker during Prohibition when the 18th Amendment restricted alcohol sales. During this time, the ladies' bathroom housed a door to this secret room supplying liquor. Anyone who imbibed exited the dark, long and narrow room with a coffee cup full of spirits to bring back to their table in another dining room. Social code dictated that when asked from where the drink came, the standard reply was: "It's a mystery to me." I adjusted a chair to line up with a place setting, then left the room.

The door to The Dungeon featured a large wooden sign that stated an epicurean quote by 18th century French gastronome Jean Anthelme Brillat-Savarin: "The Dungeon - The joys of the table belong equally to all ages, conditions, and times; they mix with all other pleasures and remain the last to console us for their loss." Even though The Dungeon creeped me out, it was a petite version of the large annex dining room with its crimson and black walls that I often frequented.

Also red and black, The 1840 Room housed photographs of the restaurant's founding Alciatore family and successive generations, like the Large Annex dining room. A miniature suit of armor stood guard in the corner protecting a 1650s Parisian cookbook and a silver duck press in the period museum. I gave the room a quick nod of approval.

I entered the gold and green Rex Room. A massive crystal chandelier illuminated the large oval table set for 25 people. The inset internal window on the left side of the room housed a mannequin wearing a gold lamé jewel-encrusted Carnival gown. All of the emerald and white china on the table looked perfect.

The Proteus Room was exactly how I left it when Elle approached me after her incident in the wine cellar last week.

As I was about to enter the Escargot Room, with its massive rudimentary artwork of a snail on the back wall, a woman's voice caught my attention. I turned, took a few steps, and waited outside of the nearby wine cellar, listening closely.

The woman's voice sang the melodious tune of "Dream a little dream of me."

Her voice. That voice. That beautiful voice practically soothed me into slumber. I could listen to that velvety sound for days. The graceful, yet haunting, musical notes mesmerized me. I lingered outside the open cellar door, not wanting to interrupt the lovely sound.

She sang some more verses.

Hearing her sing brought me to a time and place in my mind that I had only visited in my dreams. That angelic voice softened the air around me, opening my lungs. That voice, that unmistakable voice that called me home. That raspy, vampy voice lulled men to sleep. The lovely sound taught birds a new melody. That voice drowned out car horns and people talking. That voice calmed a barking dog, soothed a baby into slumber, and turned a hurricane into a soft, summer rain.

I listened with my mind, remembering. That voice used to sing to me, to calm the chaos, to comfort me, to surround me with love. Who now owned this enchanting voice that I first heard so many years ago?

I turned the corner into the wine cellar and stopped in my tracks.

Elle stood singing, her back to me, checking over the thousands of old rums, liqueurs, absinthe, and whiskey bottles in the 165-foot-long, narrow room.

"No…." a whisper escaped my lips. "It can't be…" In shock, my feet refused to move closer to her. That voice belonged to someone else I used to know, not Elle. That's how I knew her eyes. They paired with that voice. That lovely, dreamy voice that brought me such joy. What was I going to do? Elle would never understand how I know her. She would never believe me. How would I tell her? My stomach instantly filled with knots.

Elle stopped singing and quickly turned to face me, pushing a bottle of pinot grigio back into its slot. "Oh, I'm so sorry, I didn't know anyone else was down here. I'm so embarrassed. I love to sing but hate doin' it in front of people."

I stared at her, my mouth agape.

"Will, you okay?" she asked. "I'm no Aretha Franklin, but I'm not that bad, am I?"

"What?" I robotically answered, still mesmerized.

"I asked you if my singin' was that bad," Elle repeated.

"What-- No--" I acknowledged what she said, but my brain couldn't process anything. "Your voice is ... amazing," I barely uttered.

Elle blushed and dropped her head toward the floor in embarrassment. "Thank you."

Finally breaking out of my trance, I reassured her, "No, no, it's not. You're so confident otherwise, so I don't get why you're insecure about this. You sing like Ella Fitzgerald."

"Who?" Elle asked with a flutter in her voice.

"You know... Ella Fitzgerald," I quizzed her. "The blues and jazz singer from the 1950s and 60s?"

Elle blankly stared at me, her eyes unmoving.

48

"Okay, then you have to know who Louis Armstrong is, right?" I asked, exasperated and hoping that she was familiar with the most famous musician from New Orleans. "Satchmo?"

"Our airport is named after him, isn't it?" Elle asked.

I slapped a hand to my forehead. How could she be this naive in a city where music was like breathing? No one could walk a block in this town without hearing a trumpeter on the street corner or peer in art galleries full of canvases of jazz-era musicians like Mahalia Jackson, Fats Domino, and Trombone Shorty.

"Yes," I patiently replied, but still a little annoyed at her ignorance. "Our airport is named after him."

Elle pointed at me and laughed. Big belly laughs exited her mouth causing a few tears to run down her cheeks.

"That's payback for the other night," she jested. "Of course, I know who Ella Fitzgerald is. My parents *named* me after her. My mama is a piano teacher and my daddy plays trumpet at The Spotted Cat." Elle laughed again and pointed at me. "You should have seen the look on your face. I could barely hold it in."

I yielded a chuckle. "Good one," I said. "You got me."

"You walked right into that," Elle said, still laughing at me.

Elle left me, humming the rest of her song as she turned the corner and disappeared into The Tabasco Room.

That voice again. What was I going to do?

CHAPTER 6

My Darling,   *20 August, 1863*

Being the apprentice for the commission merchant is proving to be successful for me... for us. Monsieur DuBois has introduced me to many officials here. He occasionally takes me to the plantations outside the city to meet them. I want to buy you a house that big one day. Our home will be filled with happy, laughing children. My heart aches for you.

Yours forever,

51

Frédéric

"Which one of you pissed off Frédéric last night?" Chef Miguel bellowed at all of us in the kitchen early the next morning. Assistant chefs, waiters, wine stewards, busboys, and dishwashers gathered in front of him.

Darting glances and hushed murmurs inquiring the culprit bounced around the room.

"What's goin' on?" I whispered to Terrance, as we hung in the back of the large crowd of wait and kitchen staff.

"No idea. I came in the back door a few minutes ago," he quietly spoke back. "Chef Miguel sent out a text to everyone at 7:00 this mornin' sayin' to get to the restaurant ASAP."

"Who did it?" Chef Miguel demanded. His usually happy demeanor was replaced with annoyed gruff. "Frédéric's been calm for a while now and somethin' set him off."

No one stepped forward.

Terrance glared at me.

Chef Miguel blew out a disgruntled sigh. "We have to close for lunch because Frédéric came through like Katrina last night and made a mess of Hermes bar and the main dinin' room," he explained. "I know it was him because the front doors were locked and there was no

52

sign of anyone breakin' in. I reviewed the security cameras and an apparition was tearin' up the place."

Chef Miguel's large congregation hummed with side comments.

He continued, "We can't leak it to the public that our resident ghost is causin' a ruckus. Even though it might cause a business boom, we still have to clean up the mess. I'll post on the website that the fire suppressant system malfunctioned and that we'll be closed for lunch. Hopefully, with all of us here, we can get the disaster cleaned up before the dinner crowd comes at 5:30." He assigned clean-up duty to small groups one at a time.

Along with some of our coworkers, Terrance and I stepped into Hermes Bar several minutes later and collectively gasped.

Two dozen brown, wooden chairs scattered across the floor like giant Legos in a preschool room. A few tables suffered broken legs, sloping awkwardly into the black and white checkered floor. Hundreds of white, paper napkin squares smothered the mahogany bar. Clear liquid pooled in the far corner of the room. Purple and yellow fleur de lis banners that used to hang on the walls were now woven through the arms of the brass chandeliers above us. Bottles of absinthe, liqueur, and tequila were knocked down like bowling pins along the bar shelving. Sticky orange and lemon slices spelled out "FRED" on the large brass mirror above the marble fireplace.

"Watch your step," I directed Terrance as we dodged land mines of broken glass all over the floor.

"Chef Miguel wasn't kidding," Terrance said. "It's gonna take us a few hours to clean this up. It's a war zone in here. Gotta wonder what the main dinin' room is like."

"Let's get to work," I said, heading for a broom and dustpan in the nearby supply closet.

I swept the glass from the floor while Terrance mopped up a puddle of vodka. Our coworkers set chairs back up, moved out the broken tables, and cleaned up the napkins.

Terrance nodded toward the fruit signature on the mirror. "That's a new one."

I shook my head with a slight laugh.

When Elle charged into the bar, we stopped working for a moment and gazed up at her.

"Wow!" she exclaimed, surveying the scene of destruction. "Just wow."

"Now do you believe in ghosts, Elle?" Terrance pressed her, his hands gripping a wooden mop.

"Um, I..., um..." she stuttered. "No, because so many things can be explained, but this... this..." She stared at the room in awe. "Is Chef Miguel *sure* that no one broke in and did this?"

"He's sure," I insisted. "It was Frédéric."

Elle stepped over to the bar, turned away from us, and began setting the bottles of alcohol upright.

When we finished cleaning Hermes Bar three hours later, we all moved to the main dining room armed with brooms and mops to assist that cleanup crew. Most of the initial debris had been picked up by the first responders, so we reset tables, folded napkins, adjusted photos on the wall, and restocked glasses for the dinner crowd.

* * *

"What a long day," Elle sighed to me, collapsing into a dining room chair at the end of the dinner shift. Darkness seeped into the windows, casting an angelic mist from the streetlights. "Good thing I'm off tomorrow."

"You sleepin' in?" I asked her.

"Till noon," she said, closing her eyes. She rested her head against the wooden wall behind her. "But I do need to stop at a gift shop in Jackson Square in the afternoon to pick out a birthday present for my Auntie Viola."

"Well, if you want some company tomorrow, I can meet you there," I told her.

Elle slowly opened her eyes and peered at me, without moving her head. "I might take you up on that."

CHAPTER 7

My Darling,   29 August, 1863
     Vieux Carré is full of many strange and wonderful people. I hear of a voodoo priestess named Marie Laveau who parades the streets like she owns them. Les Americains go to her to cure their ails and find true love. Some people fear her abilities. I am not sure I believe it all, but it is certainly fascinating to hear. Ma chérie, I fear nothing when I think of you.
     Yours forever,

Frédéric

The next afternoon, I met Elle at the west corner of Jackson Square. Even with the high temperatures and ruthless humidity of late August, tourists came in droves to take horse-drawn carriage rides, examine artwork hung from the iron fence, and dripping sweat in the long line waiting for fresh beignets and cafe au lait at Café Du Monde on the east corner of the square. With its soaring and majestic steeples, St. Louis Cathedral held court over the lavish, green gardens and fountain.

"Are you sure you want to do this?" Elle asked. "I can't imagine an antique shop is that much fun for a guy."

"I'm sure," I said. "I'll be fine."

"Let's go then," she said, leading me through my beloved city.

Elle and I made our way along St. Peter Street, weaving around the heavy foot traffic bordering Jackson Square. Several yards ahead of us, a young father wiped sticky ice cream from his little girl's face. A retired couple sipped iced tea under the massive trees on the other side of the walkway. A dozen people gathered around a tour guide waiting to hear the background of the historic park.

The red brick Pontalba Building, with its 1840 Parisian-style row house design and second and third-story intricate iron galleries, provided shade for us.

We ducked into a small, unobtrusive shop on the sidewalk level. On the wall, framed artwork of recent Democratic Presidents playing pool invited us in.

I followed Elle around the front half of the store as she stopped and studied the eclectic cornucopia: an old plane propeller, a black vintage corded phone, a partially rusted metal sign advertising Chevy trucks. Small figurines made from upcycled metal took up occupancy on the steps of a circular staircase that once led to the second floor.

"What will your auntie like?" I asked Elle.

"She's tough to buy for because she's so finicky." Elle grazed her hand along a table of mosaic tile bowls. "She'll tell you flat out when somethin' is tacky or fake. But she's into vintage art and signs. Her house is full of them." Elle's gaze focused on an iron sculpture of a mermaid on the table, but she took a step forward without looking where she was going.

"Watch your head!" I called out to her.

Elle turned and gasped, stopping suddenly within inches of colliding with a low-hanging chandelier that was for sale.

"Yikes!" she said. "We already cleaned up enough glass yesterday."

"Right. Have you ever been in that antique shop on Royal Street?" I asked her. "The one across from Café Beignet?"

"Yes," Elle replied. "That place has massive, gorgeous chandeliers. But I could never buy one, not when they cost more than my car."

We examined the vintage art along the perimeter wall of the shop.

"I'm not findin' anything I like for my auntie." Elle sighed at the oil canvasses of smiling children and landscapes. "Nothin' is catchin' my eye."

Ahead of Elle, I headed toward the aviation-themed corner of the store.

"What about this?" I called to Elle, pointing to an old green and red metal sign advertising five-cent Coca-Cola. "You said she likes vintage signs."

No answer.

"Elle?" I said, finally glancing back to where she remained, studying a framed vintage photo.

In ten steps, I stood behind her, curious to see what captured her attention.

"This picture… it's so fascinatin', so peculiar," Elle said, though her body faced away from me. "It's gotta be from the mid-1800s." She stood motionless, still mesmerized by the photo.

I peered over her shoulder and quietly gasped. Words left me as I stared at the old, grayed framed photo portraying a young man in a dark suit and top hat leaning against the rail at the bottom of the staircase of the Beauregard-Keyes House on Chartres Street. He was tall and thin with a dark mustache and beard, but the rest of the details of his face faded away in the aged photo.

In an attempt to hide my shock at seeing the photo, I suggested, "It's great, but you don't really want to get that for your aunt, do you? You said she's into vintage stuff. I found a great old Coke sign you might like over there." I pointed toward the other end of the shop, verbally nudging Elle away.

"Yeah… yeah… you're right," she finally fully acknowledged me. Elle turned to face me. "Where did you say that Coke sign was?"

"Over there," I said, cocking my head in the opposite direction.

A few minutes later, Elle and I stood at the cash register. An older gentleman with white hair and wire-framed glasses approached us from behind the counter.

"Did you find everythin' you like, miss?" he asked Elle, taking the sign from her hands.

"Yes, sir," she said. "I love comin' into your store. I always see somethin' new. Sometimes old."

"What did you discover this time?" he asked her while ringing up her purchase.

"An old black and white photo on your back wall," Elle said.

"Ah, yes," the man said, stopping his multitasking. "The one of the gentleman in the suit in front of the

60

Beauregard-Keyes House. My mama volunteered there at Christmas time durin' World War II. Servin' the boys turkey with all the fixins'."

"But do you know who the man is in the picture?" Elle wanted to know. "He looked familiar to me."

"No, miss, I'm 'fraid I don't. You might want to check with The Historic New Orleans Collection over on Royal. They pretty much know everythin' about this town," the shop owner replied. He rang up the Coke sign. "That'll be $42.79, please."

Elle dug a credit card out of her wallet and ran it through the shop owner's point of sale pad.

Five minutes later, Elle and I found our way along St. Peter Street and headed toward Decatur Street. Ahead, the Mississippi River taunted us with her tales of 300 years of industrialization, culinary, music, and voodoo culture in the Crescent City.

"Are you hungry at all?" Elle asked me, gazing down Decatur toward the long line at Café Du Monde. "I could use a beignet."

"Nah, I'm fine," I said. "But I'll keep you company while you wait in line."

Elle grinned at me. Her wide eyes sparkled. Those lovely pools of azure. Those wonderful eyes mesmerized me. I still wasn't sure how to tell her how I knew her.

"You're one of the good ones," she said.

I blushed.

CHAPTER 8

My Darling,   *6 September, 1863*

While I was out strolling today along Rue St. Louis, I saw a young woman on the street who resembled you. She had long blonde hair and wide blue eyes, like you. She was not allowed to catch my eye because she was with an escort. Shortly after, I ducked into a restaurant called Antoine's. We could have our wedding dinner there when you finally arrive here. It's lovely and would be perfect for us. I miss you so much, ma chérie.

Yours forever,

Frédéric

"How was your *shoppin' trip* with Elle yesterday?" Terrance asked me as we set up a table of ten for an upcoming dinner reservation in the main dining room.

"We had a good time," I told him. "We went to an antique shop and she bought a birthday gift for her auntie."

"Sounds *exciting*," Terrance sarcassed. "Looks like you've been friend-zoned."

As I set up a place setting, I glowered at him.

"What?" he said, noticing my hard stare. "Why are you lookin' at me like that?"

"It's Elle," I told him. "I know her."

"What? What do you mean you *know* her?" Terrance asked. "You mean you've met her before?"

"No, not exactly," I said.

"Then how?"

"The other day she was singin' in the wine cellar," I replied. "I've listened to that voice a thousand times before. It used to calm me on my worst days. I fell asleep to that wonderful sound."

"You're serious?"

"Yes," I said. "Dead serious. But I don't think she knows, just by the way she talks."

"You tellin' her?" Terrance pressed.

"I don't know yet," I pondered. "But, if you think of a way, tell me because I don't have a clue."

"Sure thing, brother."

Chef Miguel sauntered into the room and interrupted us. "Do you two want to work Bourbon Street tonight?" When the weather allowed it, our staff took turns manning a table with takeaway food from five to seven at night in the middle of the 400 block of Bourbon Street.

"Sure, Chef," Terrance answered for both of us. "That'd be great."

"What are you servin' tonight?" I asked.

"Chilled shrimp over sweet potato vichyssoise and mini Baked Alaska," Chef Miguel replied. "Head into the kitchen. Georgia and Charles are in there and will help you get set up."

* * *

An hour later, after waiting for a mini-parade to march through Bourbon Street for some obscure saint's day festival, Terrance and I stood behind a linen-skirted table full of metal chafing dishes filled with cold shrimp and soup. On the ground, a small fridge chilled plastic bourbon glasses of Baked Alaska.

Contrary to popular belief, Bourbon Street was not named for the drink. Louisiana was originally a French colony in the 1690s. Frenchman Jean Baptiste Le Moyne de Bienville founded New Orleans in 1718. He named the streets after the French royal houses and Catholic saints of that period. Bourbon Street honored France's ruling family, the House of Bourbon.

Along with a couple of our other coworkers, Georgia situated herself at the front of the table collecting cash before Terrance and I filled the orders.

Small groups of tourists filled the street. The local police barricaded the road to prevent vehicle traffic at night. Rock music from the nearby open-walled bars blared into the street. Pink, yellow, and green neon signs advertising frozen drinks and voodoo flickered on. A few people lingered on the second-story galleries above us. The stomach-churning funk of urine, rotten seafood, and garbage permeated from the infamously rowdy street into our noses.

The sun dipped down over the buildings heading toward Dauphine Street. In a couple of hours, Bourbon Street would be filled with wall-to-wall partygoers searching out watered-down budget drinks and loose women who might lift their shirt for a few strands of cheap plastic beads.

"I don't mind comin' down here this time of day," Terrance lamented. "But those crazy tourists later on won't appreciate this city for what it is. All they want to do is party. I'm all for partyin' but the true music is further down a few blocks and on the side streets."

"That's why we go to One Eyed Jacks," I said. "You and I both know that the tourists don't know about that place because it doesn't have a big flashy sign connin' them in."

Terrance scooped a plastic bowl of soup, dropped a matching spoon in the dish, and handed it to a woman in front of him. "Here you go, ma'am."

"This is perfect for a hot summer evening," she said. "I love coming to NOLA." She slid a napkin off the table, cupped the bowl with it, and wandered off down the bustling street.

"Yankee," Terrance scoffed. Small beads of sweat trickled down his dark face as dusk encroached upon us. Even at night, the suffocating humidity gave little reprieve.

For the next two hours, Terrance served cool soup and chilled shrimp while I discreetly made sure all of his table provisions were constantly stocked. Even though we weren't within the confines of Antoine's, we were still expected to maintain fine dining service.

A shriek from a passerby drew my attention.

"Will, what are you lookin' at?" Terrance followed my gaze toward the Conti Street intersection a hundred feet away.

Out of the corner of my eye, I caught sight of an older woman who was in her mid-60s. Even though the street was reaching capacity with foot traffic, she stood by herself 20 feet away in the middle of the sidewalk, crying.

"I need to help her," I told Terrance. "She's in trouble. And everyone else around here is ignoring her."

"No, Will, don't," he called to me. "She might think you're..."

Before Terrance finished his sentence, I maneuvered myself around the tables and rushed over to the woman.

Above me, blue and purple neon signs flickered at a rapid pace until they fizzled out. Music stopped playing. Partygoers hushed. The warm breeze around us halted. For a few rare moments, Bourbon Street was eerily still and quiet. A few seconds later, as if nothing happened, the street came to life again.

As I approached the woman with ease, I quietly spoke, "Excuse me, ma'am. I don't mean to bother you, but are you okay? Is there anythin' I can do to help you?"

"I don't know what to do," she cried. Her body shook in hysterics. She examined the crowd around us as tears trickled down her face.

"What happened?" I asked her.

"Right before the lights and music went off, some guy stole my purse. It had everything in it." She took a step away from me, carefully scanning the street over my shoulder. "My keys, my wallet, my phone. I have nothing. I can't even call the police."

I spied over my shoulder to see if any officers were nearby. A figure in a blue uniform stood sentry a block away. I shook my head knowing that I was closer.

"It's okay, I'll help you," I consoled her, trying hard not to invade her personal space and frightening her further. "Are you hurt? Come with me. I'll take you to the policeman over there." Unsure if she would accept my help, I still felt the need to assist her in any way I could.

Her hands shook as she spoke, "Thank you. I'm not hurt. The mugger snagged my purse from my shoulder and took off. My friend and I split up at lunch and we planned to meet up for a late dinner at Mr. B's and now I can't even call her."

Terrance left the food table and joined us as I guided the woman toward the cop. As we approached, he pulled a small tablet out of a pocket to take her statement.

"You two are so kind," the woman sniffed.

While the woman talked to the police officer, Terrance turned to me.

"You got lucky this time," he whispered to me. "She could have thought you were a total creep. Especially in this town."

CHAPTER 9

My Darling,   15 September, 1863

Thank you so much for the beautiful silk bowtie you sent me. I treasure it as I treasure you. I will wear it when I attend a ball at Ormond Plantation when I travel with Monsieur DuBois on the night after next. I wish you could attend with me. I miss dancing with you and feeling you in my arms.

Yours forever,
Frédéric

"How was Bourbon Street last night?" Elle asked Terrance and me the next day while we stocked the server station with silverware and crystal water glasses.

"The usual," I said with a shrug.

"The *usual*?" Terrance jested me with a slight scoff. "Not really."

"Why? What happened?" Elle wanted to know, pausing midway putting a glass away on the bottom shelf.

"Will played hero to a woman who got mugged on Bourbon Street." Terrance pointed to me.

"You helped her too," I replied. "I can't take all the credit."

"Wow… you two are the modern-day version of the kindness of strangers," Elle joked.

"Doesn't everyone help out like that?" I questioned.

"Um, no," Elle said. "I bet that woman stood there for a good 10 minutes before you saw her, because no one else cared enough to lift their heads out of their phones. I'm sure she appreciated what you did for her."

"Well, that's how I was brought up," I told her. "To assist people when they need it."

"Speakin' of assistance," Elle said to me. "Do you want to come with me to The Historic New Orleans Collection on our next day off? It's right around the corner from here. When I unexpectedly got off early last night, I went back to the antique shop and bought that old photo I liked."

70

"What about me? You dissin' me, girl?" Terrance balked with a broad smile, pointing to himself.

"I didn't think a big, tough guy like you would be interested in a history museum." She punched him lightly in the bicep. "But you can come too if you want," she told him.

* * *

After lunch a few days later, Elle, Terrance, and I met on the sidewalk in front of The Historic New Orleans Collection. The salmon-colored two-story reference building nestled between a vintage clothing shop and a women's Parisian boutique. Tall green wooden double doors invited us in from the summer heat that licked our faces.

As we pushed inside, a blast of arctic chill encircled us in the red-carpeted foyer.

"I swear when it's hot outside, I need a sweater inside," Elle stated, clutching the framed photo in a canvas bag.

"Hello, can I help you?" A lanky blonde woman in a pink floral dress met us in the foyer. She was a good head taller than Elle.

"Yes, ma'am," Elle spoke, pulling the picture out of the bag. "I was wonderin' if you can tell me more about this photo."

"Do you mind if I take a closer look?" The woman held her palm out.

"Yes, please." Elle tenderly placed the frame in the woman's hand.

The woman examined it closely, a few inches from her face. "Obviously this is the Beauregard-Keyes House. But I'm not sure who the man is, because it isn't General Beauregard and it's obviously not Frances Keyes. General Beauregard lived there in the late 1860s and, judging by the war lapel pin on this man's suit, this photo was taken a few years before that."

"Do you have records back that far?" Elle asked her.

"Yes, of course, we do," the pleasant woman said. "Lots of 19th Century immigrants came through the Port of New Orleans. Follow me."

"You are really obsessed with this photo, aren't you?" I whispered to Elle as we trailed behind the woman.

"I can't explain it," Elle quietly spoke back. "Somethin' about this man. His mustache and beard... I feel like I've met him before. Maybe I'm related somehow?"

"But the man in the photo is white," Terrance interrupted. "And you're--"

"A quarter white." Elle glared at him with daggers for eyes. "My Grannie Betsy is white."

Terrance shut his mouth and we all followed the woman into the large research room. A dozen mahogany tables with matching chairs filled out the area receiving sunlight from the two-story palladium windows. On the other side of the room, twenty-foot tall bookcases stretched from floor to ceiling. A spiral staircase led diligent researchers to the top.

"You'll find the census records from the mid-1800s up there," the woman said, pointing over her shoulder toward the middle of the bookcases.

Elle gasped. "Look, you two don't have to help me," she told Terrance and me. "This might take a while so if you have somethin' else you need to do, you don't have to stay."

"I can stay for a little bit," Terrance said. "I don't have any other plans until later tonight."

"Why? You have a date?" I jested.

"Yup," he said. "Met her when I was workin' in our bar the other night. Some jerk bailed on her."

"You swooped in and rescued her?" I asked.

"Like you did with the lady on Bourbon Street." He winked at me.

"I'm among local heroes," Elle jested.

After two hours of flipping through pages of books reviewing names and addresses, Elle collapsed into a wooden chair in front of Terrance and me.

"I'm beat. My eyes might pop out of my head," she sighed. "We've gone through all these books and can't find anythin' that makes sense. We have nothin' to go on except that he's a white man standin' in front of a now-famous house. He could be anyone!"

"Don't give up, Elle," I told her. "I'm sure one day you'll figure out who he is."

"I sure hope so," she sighed. "Because I can't get over how familiar he is."

CHAPTER 10

My Darling,   26 September, 1863

The portrait of you was completed today, a month earlier than expected. I hung it above the mantel in the parlour so that I can see your beautiful face every day. Every morning when I wake, I imagine you next to me. I miss you so much, ma chérie.

Yours forever,
Frédéric

Ten minutes later, Elle and I parted ways with Terrance on the sidewalk so that he could get ready for his date.

"I could use a drink after all this," Elle told me. "I know you don't drink, but do you want to join me?" She clutched the canvas bag holding the antique photo in her hands.

"Sure."

"If you don't mind walkin' a few blocks, let's go to Fritzel's," Elle said.

"I love that place," I told her. "It's a hole in the wall, but the music is great."

We headed left on Royal Street weaving our way around oncoming bicyclists, delivery men pushing metal wheeled dollies, tourists taking pictures, and street musicians with open trumpet cases at their feet. Cars coming down the one-way street honked at each other. Lively conversations from nearby restaurants echoed out open doors and spilled onto the sidewalk.

As St. Louis Cathedral came into our sights across the street, local artists displayed their wares along the iron fence of the massive church's courtyard. Unframed black and white sketches of Louis Armstrong, Prince, and Muhammad Ali took center stage.

"Come on." Elle stepped ahead of me, waiting for traffic to clear so that she could cross the busy street.

"For what?" I balked. "You *like* that tacky art?"

"No, it's not the art I want to see," Elle explained, studying the passing cars in front of her, waiting for a break. "Faulkner House Books is down Pirate Alley." Local legend stated that the alley earned its name from the influx of pirates in the 1700s who entered the city from the Mississippi River a quarter-mile away. These days, a chaplain married couples with a quick elopement in the infamous throughway. "The bookstore is still open. It's a mecca for fine literature and rare books."

"You didn't see enough books at the historic collection?" I asked her.

"No way," Elle replied. "I hoard old books."

Between a gap in cars, we crossed the street and headed toward the bookstore.

Moments later, the hinges on the enormous door creaked as we stepped inside the former home of William Faulkner. Floor-to-ceiling bookcases full of multicolored spines welcomed us. Brass chandeliers hung from the ceiling. In the middle of the room, stacks of books overflowed on a large table.

"Hello-o-o..." Elle called in the empty room as she roamed toward the middle. I followed her.

An older man with wire-rimmed glasses and a bushy mustache appeared from the off-limits hallway. He wore a white button-down linen shirt and tan trousers. A few grey curls accentuated his dark hair.

77

"Miss Elle!" he gushed, heading toward her. A broad smile formed on his soft face. "I haven't seen you in ages."

"Hello, Mr. Howard." Elle embraced him. Then she motioned toward me. "I'd like you to meet…" Suddenly, the lights flickered on and off a few times.

"That's weird," Mr. Howard said, scrutinizing the ceiling fixtures. "We aren't expectin' any thunderstorms for a few days. Maybe it's a brownout because it's been so hot lately?" His attention focused back on Elle. "Anyway, what were you sayin'?"

"This is my friend Will," Elle pointed over her shoulder to me. "We work together at Antoine's."

I gave a quick wave to the bookshop owner. "Good to meet you."

"How's she doin' at work?" the genteel man said to me.

"She's a natural," I said, with a smile. "She's great."

"Good to hear," Mr. Howard said, and then focused back on Elle. "How are your parents?"

"They're fine." Elle turned to me. "Mr. Howard and my daddy played together at The Spotted Cat on Frenchman Street when I was younger. Then he'd come by the house and they'd have a jam session. Along with my mom, they taught me everythin' I know about music."

"And now she comes here for my books," he said to me. "I have some new ones from Derek Walcott if you want to check them out."

"Let me take a look," Elle replied. She stepped toward him as he directed her to the small collection on a nearby table.

Mr. Howard turned back to me. "Do you see anythin' you like?"

"I can't even figure out where to start," I replied, taking in the massive collection. Then a familiar scent distracted me. "Is someone smokin' a pipe in here?"

Mr. Howard chuckled. "No, that's our resident ghost, William Faulkner."

"Seriously?" I laughed.

"Yes," Mr. Howard replied. "And I can't keep any attractive women on staff because of him." He shook his head in indignation.

"Why not?" I asked.

"Because he is, was, a terrible letch and these women said they felt inappropriate touchin' when no one else was around," Mr. Howard explained. "It got so bad that many of them quit within a couple of weeks. It's not like I can fire him. And he won't go away on his own."

"Did you hear that Elle?" I called to her. She was engrossed in the Walcott books. "A ghost haunts this place too. And he cops a feel."

"Yeah well, I still don't believe in 'em," she said to me, without shifting her body in my direction.

I turned back to Mr. Howard with a smug expression on my face. "She doesn't believe that Antoine's is haunted even though everyone else there has seen and talked to the ghost."

Elle scoffed, again without glancing up.

We perused the book shop for the next hour, taking in the works of James Joyce, Stewart O'Nan, and Louisiana native son Walker Percy. The pipe scent tickled my nose as Mr. Howard led Elle and me into a small room filled with walls of books that could have been a parlor.

"What are you doin'?" I said to Elle as she pressed down the bottom trim of her light blue tank top.

"My shirt flipped up and I pushed it down," she explained. "Must have been a blast of air from the air conditioning actin' up."

I smiled as Elle left the former parlor and headed toward the front room again.

"I know you are here," I said out loud in the empty sitting room. "And I know you groped Elle a few moments ago."

"Don't worry, she'll know I'm real soon enough," a man's ghostly voice answered me.

CHAPTER 11

My Darling,   5 October, 1863
    Your letter arrived yesterday, and your wonderful perfume still lingered on it. I sniffed it many times this morning to remind myself of you. You are my life, my breath. The weather here is finally bearable, but still warmer than summers in France. You will not have to wear an overcoat, but I promise I will keep you warm if you get cold.
    Yours forever,
    Frédéric

"Thanks for goin' with me to the bookstore yesterday," Elle said to me as we prepped for the lunch shift in the main dining room. She stacked clean glasses on the shelf while I inspected the silverware, making sure the silver oyster forks were arranged properly.

"It was fun," I said. "I had a good time. Sorry we never made it to Fritzel's."

"Maybe we'll go there on our next day off?" she offered.

"Sure," I said. "Speakin' of goin' out, whatever happened with that guy from One Eyed Jacks?"

"Well…" she explained, "as you and Terrance suspected, he was flattered…"

"I sense a 'but'," I interrupted.

"But… he told me he had a girlfriend," Elle sighed. "At least he was upfront with me and didn't play games. Last year, this guy Matt texted me all day every day for six weeks straight and then ghosted me." She shook her head at the memory. "What a jerk."

"That's too bad. His loss," I replied. "You're a catch." Instantly, I wanted to stuff those words back in my big mouth.

"Thank you," Elle said and looked at me askance. "But you know I don't date co-workers."

"I know." I was thankful for Elle's rule, but I still had to find a way to tell her how I knew her. Once I told her, everything would change.

I left Elle and found Terrance setting tables in the large annex dining room.

"What are you doin'?" he asked.

"I came to help you," I answered, as I grabbed a handful of silverware.

"No, I mean what are you doin' with Elle?" he corrected himself. "Have you figured how you're tellin' her that you know her?"

I shook my head. "Not a clue, man."

"I'm sure you'll figure it out," Terrance said. "Did you see you're assigned to Hermes Bar for dinner tonight?"

"Yeah, that'll be good. I haven't worked in there for a while," I replied.

"Speakin' of Hermes, how was your date the other night?" I asked him while putting finishing touches on a table.

"I had a good time and I think she did too," Terrance said. "Her name is Rachel. I met her at Jacques-Imo's for drinks and crawfish."

"You seein' her again?" I pressed.

"Yeah, I invited her out with us to One Eyed Jacks the next time we go."

* * *

At the beginning of happy hour, a couple of dozen people settled around Hermes Bar with plates full of po'boys, shrimp remoulade, and crawfish bisque. Shorts-wearing patrons liked to come in for more casual bites and a less formal scene than the other fancier dining areas of the restaurant.

A 30ish man dressed in a blue golf shirt and black trousers sat at the far end of the bar. He noshed on a soft-shell crab po'boy and sipped on a bottle of Abita Imperial Stout, occasionally glancing at the TV above the marble mantle.

Two stools down from him, an attractive late 20s blonde wore a flowy white tank dress and laid a small purple purse on top of the bar. An older couple sat to her left. The young woman ordered a Lemon Sunshine from Charles, the bartender.

Charles was in his 50s, with a headful of silver hair. He had served libations at Antoine's for a couple of decades. When Katrina hit, he and his wife lost their house in Mid-City and temporarily moved to Houston and stayed with their grown son. Five months later, we welcomed him back with open arms.

"Would you like to order food, too?" Charles asked the pretty blonde.

"Yes, that'd be great," she answered with a sweet drawl. Charles handed her a menu from behind the bar.

I huddled next to Charles several feet away so that the woman could make her dinner choice without us hovering over her. "Is she by herself?" I nodded to her.

"Yes," Charles replied. "I think so."

"And that man over there?" I motioned to the man in the blue shirt at the end of the bar.

"Yep," Charles said. "I've seen him here a few times. Orders a po'boy and a beer. Seems like a nice fella, but generally keeps to himself. I've never seen anyone else with him."

"Hmmm..." The corners of my mouth curved up into a slight smile.

A minute later, Charles strode over to the woman.

"What're you hungry for?" he asked her, with a broad grin.

"I'll take soufflé potatoes with a cup of gumbo," she said.

"Both good choices," Charles replied. "Is anyone joinin' you tonight?"

"No," she said and lowered her head. "Just me. I've always wanted to eat here, but never had the nerve to come by myself."

"Well, I'm glad you're here," Charles said. "If you need anythin', you let me know. My name is Charles."

"Thank you, Charles," she replied.

Charles stepped away from her to place the order on the point-of-sale monitor.

Out of the corner of my eye, the man at the end of the bar took notice of the attractive blonde woman. He swiftly looked her up and down and a slight smile formed on his face. When she opened her purse to pull out her phone and turned in his direction, he quickly put his focus on the TV.

She tapped her phone in her hand and stopped. She gazed at the man who tugged at her attention and stared at him over the top of her phone.

Charles sauntered over to me.

"You seein' this?" I asked him. "That guy was checking her out, then turned away when she faced his direction. Then she couldn't take her eyes off of him. But neither of them will make a move to talk to the other."

"I know how you like to help people out, Will," Charles said. "But be discreet. You don't want to scare them off. Then they'll never get together." He turned away from me to clean some dirty glasses in the small sink behind the bar.

"Good point," I replied. I studied them, figuring out my best options to play matchmaker. "Got it," I said, more to myself than to Charles.

I headed for the air conditioning controls on the wall on the far side of the room. I adjusted the buttons on the small screen, turned myself in the direction of the man and the woman, and waited.

Within moments, the pretty blonde shuddered. She crossed her arms, staving off the cool breeze that pushed at her. Her lightweight dress didn't provide much comfort. The older gentleman in the wooden bar stool to her left didn't seem to be affected by the cold blast of air as he drowned in conversation with his wife. The young woman perused the room, the area near capacity with other patrons. The only empty chair was to her right, next to the lone man, but still in the path of the gust of cold air.

Out of options, the woman climbed out of her seat and hesitated before she settled into the one next to her, accidentally bumping the man.

"I'm so sorry," she said to him. "I didn't mean to bump you."

"It's okay," he told her, finally able to fully gaze at her.

"Is this seat taken?" she asked him.

"No, I'm by myself. "Have a seat." He motioned to the empty chair. "What happened to your other spot?"

"I don't know," she replied, settling herself into the tall bar stool next to him. "All of a sudden, the AC kicked on and a blast of cold air came at me. I was freezing."

"Well, you know that's how summers are in the South. It might be 95 outside, but you need a jacket inside. I hope you're warmer over here," he told her. "My name's Frank." He extended his hand to her.

"I'm Natalie," she said, taking his hand.

As Frank and Natalie talked, I readjusted the air conditioning to its normal state and stepped over to Charles.

"Way to go, Will," he told me, nodding toward Frank and Natalie. "You're quite the matchmaker."

CHAPTER 12

My Darling,   18 October, 1863
    This morning, I attended Mass at The Cathedral of St. Louis, named after our former king. I hope that we can have our wedding ceremony there. It is a magnificent building. The clock in the bell tower chimes on the hour and it is a lovely sound. I miss the sound of your voice. When you speak, you calm me from whatever worries me. I miss you so much that my heart aches.
    Yours forever,

Frédéric

A few days later, Elle found me in the kitchen shucking oysters with Chef Miguel.

"Even though I've lived here all my life," she said, while examining our work, "I'll still never get used to eatin' a raw oyster." She crossed her eyes and bent her mouth like she was possessed by a voodoo demon.

"It's an acquired taste," Chef Miguel said. "But these little buggers have been the highlight of our menu ever since the days of John Rockefeller. Antoine's son Jules created them in 1889 when we had a shortage of escargot and he subbed in local oysters. They became an instant favorite."

"Why do you make the sauce green, Chef?" I inquired, a sealed oyster in one hand and a small knife in the other.

"It's the color of money." He winked at me.

Elle and I both barked a laugh.

"Hey, Chef," Elle said. "You've worked in the Quarter a long time, haven't you?"

"Most of my life," he answered, with a broad grin. "I couldn't imagine bein' anywhere else. I love this city."

"So, you *know* people?" Elle asked, her mermaid-colored eyes drawing down.

"Hold on... What kind of people are you talkin' about?" I interrupted, unsure if she meant something criminal or underground. Despite local skepticism, voodoo practice ran rampant in the mystical city. Crime and muggings prevented solo women from walking the streets at night.

"No, it's not like that." Elle read my thoughts, then turned back to Chef Miguel. "I mean do you know someone who can help me figure out who a man is in an old photo I recently bought from an antique shop?"

"You've already been to the historic collection?" Chef asked her.

"Yes." Elle pointed to me. "We went with Terrance and spent two hours searchin' through their books and came up empty."

"What's the picture of?" Chef Miguel pressed.

"It's a younger man standin' in front of the Beauregard-Keyes House," Elle answered. "The nice woman at the historic collection thinks the picture was taken around the Civil War. Somethin' about the lapel pin on the man's jacket."

"I have just the person for you," Chef Miguel said while shucking a handful of oysters. He mastered the process so well that it was second nature to him. "Go talk to Barney at Keil's Antiques on Royal Street. He's a porter there. He knows everythin' about this town."

"Isn't that the place with the chandeliers that cost more than my house?" Elle asked with wide, cool eyes.

"Yes, but don't be intimidated," Chef Miguel replied. "Barney helped me find an antique salt cellar there for $45. He's been workin' there for almost 80 years. If he doesn't know about your picture, no one else will."

"It's worth a shot," Elle said. "Will, want to come with me again?"

"I wouldn't miss it," I replied.

Chef Miguel interjected, "Tell Barney I sent you. And he knows that his lunch here is always on the house."

* * *

On our next day off, Elle and I met in front of Keil's. Tourists wandered around us on Royal Street. Large, forest green awnings decorated the sidewalk-level windows of the three-story red brick building. Massive glass and bronze lanterns flanked the edges of the shop that shared the block with other antique proprietors. A metal fire escape connected the second and third floors above us.

I followed Elle through glass doors embossed with iron fleurs de lis. The whole shop illuminated in a yellow haze from the dozens of crystal chandeliers that hung from the ceiling. Knee-high bronze statues of Greek women dressed in togas greeted us. Eighteenth and 19th century pieces of art, furniture, and jewelry highlighted the front room.

A middle-aged couple stood at the glass counter talking to a female antiquarian.

"Let's find Barney," Elle said. She carried her portrait in a cloth tote bag over her shoulder. "He shouldn't be hard to find. I mean, how many men in their 90s could be workin' here?"

Elle led me through small rooms filled with French provincial armoires, hand-carved mahogany bed sets, and intricate gold mirrors.

We found an older gentleman with thin white hair adjusting a silver tea service on top of a century-old walnut dining table. He wore a navy-blue three-piece suit with a matching bow tie. Behind him, a mammoth china cabinet housed English early 19th century multicolored ironstone plates.

"Excuse me, sir," Elle said to him. "Are you Barney?"

"Yes, I am," he replied. "What can I help you with, miss?" He turned slowly to face Elle, but only because his mature bones couldn't keep up with his still-fresh mind.

Elle pulled the old portrait from her bag and laid it flat in her palm. "My name is Elle and I work over at Antoine's. Chef Miguel sent me to find you. I was wonderin' if you could help me figure out who this man is."

"Your Chef is a fine gentleman." Barney pulled a pair of glasses from his suit pocket and perched them on his nose.

"May I?" he said to Elle.

"Please." She handed him the picture then gazed at me while Barney studied it inches from his face.

"The pin on the man's suit is from the War of Northern Aggression," Barney explained, not looking up.

"Yes," Elle answered. "That's what the woman at the historic collection told us. But that's all she knew."

"This man is French," Barney said.

"How can you tell?" Elle asked.

"The suit he is wearin' has a coat, waistcoat, and trousers," Barney said. "The French wore their suits like that back then. Not the Spanish or the Americans. His waistcoat is not buttoned but instead left open to show the vest. Also, his coat falls straight through the center front. He is dressed nicely, so he is well employed."

Barney cleared his throat then continued. "He is not wearin' a weddin' ring, so he is single. Possibly waitin' for his bride-to-be to arrive by boat through the port."

I gasped at the nonagenarian's deduction.

Elle glared at me wondering why I gasped. I was sure she was on to me.

Barney continued talking to Elle, "The chain attached to the man's pocket would link to a pocket watch. If we had that watch, we would know this man's name because most pocket watches were engraved back then with initials and sometimes full names."

94

He lifted his head to face Elle. "My best guess is this man lived in the Quarter. The French called it Vieux Carré back then and all of the streets were called *rue* because the French insisted. Royal Street that we're standin' on was called Rue Royale back then. Most French Creole did not cross Canal Street because they didn't want to mix with the unrefined Americans who settled closer to the Garden District."

"Which explains why he is standin' in front of the Beauregard-Keyes House," Elle deduced. "Because it's in the Quarter."

"Yes, that house is on Chartres Street," Barney replied. "Do you know why none of the French Quarter streets cross Canal Street?"

"No, why?" Elle wanted to know.

"Because," Barney explained, "the French wouldn't allow it. When the Americans came here, the French were fine livin' with the Spanish. You'll see that in a lot of French Quarter architecture. But the French refused to mingle with the crude Americans or the English. They wanted the division of Canal Street to be obvious. Canal Street was the neutral-ground meetin' place of the contentious cultures so they could do business without clashing. Canal Street is one of the widest streets in the country because of that."

"I always wondered why Royal Street became St. Charles and Decatur became Magazine once they met Canal," Elle said, with a smirk. "Now it makes sense."

"Is there anythin' else you want to know, Miss Elle?" Barney asked.

"No, sir," Elle replied with a smile. "You've been a great help. Thank you so much."

"If you have any other questions, come back and find me." Barney handed the photo back to Elle and she shook his hand in return. "Tell Chef Miguel I'll be in for lunch next week."

I followed Elle toward the front of the store.

"We have a single French man who lived in the Quarter around the Civil War," Elle stated, as we left the shop. "We are a little bit further than we were, but I still don't know the man's name." Elle paused on the sidewalk, realizing what she said. "Don't even say it. I don't want to hear it."

"I didn't say a word," I gloated as if I knew the answer to every question that ran through her head.

"He looks so familiar to me," Elle sighed. Her wide, pool-blue eyes warmed me like they had a thousand times before. "I can't figure it out."

I figured out how I knew Elle. But I couldn't tell her yet.

CHAPTER 13

My Darling,   26 October, 1863

Thank you for the beautiful silk handkerchiefs. I will keep them in my inside pocket, next to my heart. As I was strolling to work this morning, I passed a house heading west on Rue Royale that made me think of you. A doctor and his wife live there. He erected a wrought iron fence with carved corn stalks at the top of each spindle to help remind his wife of the cornfields she left behind in Iowa to *move here with him. Please believe I will do anything like this for you, to make you happy. I know you are leaving your family behind when you come to be with me. I will make it up to you. I promise you.*

Yours forever,
Frédéric

Elle and I meandered down Royal Street. Few places on Earth were like New Orleans where jazz musicians, inebriated tourists, exotic dancers, priests, local politicians, drag queens, and antique dealers could all be neighbors, much less get along. In this city, self-indulgence was inherited, and imbibing was a refined pursuit. A group of women huddled on the sidewalk in front of us, pointing and talking as if they were figuring out which shop to go to next.

"Did your auntie like the vintage Coke sign you bought her?" I asked Elle. We headed north toward Conti Street passing a pink and white two-story antique shop on our left.

"Yes, she loved it," Elle said. "Thank you so much for findin' it."

A bald man in black trousers, a black suit vest, and a black server's apron crossed the sidewalk directly in front of Elle, nearly knocking her to the pavement. She shook herself off and cursed under her breath.

"I'm so sorry, miss," he gushed, grasping her elbow in an attempt to set her straight again. "I didn't even see you. I'm so sorry."

"It's okay," Elle said, facing him. "I'm fine. Will would have broken my fall." She laughed at her joke.

"Will?" the man replied, a confused expression on his face. "Who's Will?"

"My friend...." Elle started to say, glancing around and realizing I wasn't next to her. "... who was standin' right here. I swear he was here a minute ago."

"Ah, well," the man said, probably thinking Elle had too much to drink. "I'm glad you're alright. Have a good day." With that, he turned and headed in the opposite direction.

"Will?" Elle called for me.

I emerged from the open door of a nearby rare coin shop.

"Where did you go?" she asked. "Some waiter nearly knocked me down because he wasn't watchin' where he was going."

"Are you okay?" I avoided her question.

"Yeah, I'm fine," she said. "But when I turned around, you were gone."

"I wanted to check somethin' out at the coin shop," I told her. "Sorry I missed all the fun."

"It's fine," Elle replied, in sarcasm.

"Where do you want to head now?" I nodded toward the narrow street.

"I don't need to go anywhere else," Elle told me. "I know it might sound odd, but I like strollin' through the Quarter and takin' everythin' in. I've lived in New Orleans all my life and can't imagine bein' anywhere else."

"Me too," I said. "I fell in love with it the moment I got here."

"I don't think I ever asked you where you're from," Elle replied.

"I'm from Marignane," I said.

"You mean the Marigny," Elle corrected me.

"Yeah, somethin' like that," I laughed. "I swear I hear different accents from different neighborhoods around here. Guess it depends where you live."

We plodded a couple more blocks north on Royal, passing more antique shops, vintage clothing boutiques, cafés, and custom jewelry stores. Royal Street was considered the antique mecca of the South. As we passed restaurants, wonderful aromas of seafood gumbo, freshly baked bread, and sweet pralines swelled our noses.

After making a right on St. Peter Street, we headed toward the plaza between the cathedral and Jackson Square. Tourists filled the immediate area.

"Come this way. It's a shortcut. There's less traffic." Elle directed me as she made a quick left into Cabildo Alley hugged by a handful of patio tables under the red awning of a gelateria. Four orange metal planters on the sidewalk overflowed with green vines and white flowers. Even though we were a few steps away from lively St. Peter Street, the quaint alley gave a welcoming serenity. The red brick buildings above us provided cool shade from the sweltering August sun.

"Look, Elle." I pointed to a painted wooden sign hanging in front of a storefront that read `Real Estate Office`. Below it, an additional sign in red block letters said `Haunted`. "Antoine's isn't the only one exploitin' the fact that their place is haunted."

Elle scoffed. "That's to attract gullible tourists."

"You saw the damage that Frédéric caused and you still don't believe our restaurant is haunted?" I countered.

"Ehh." Elle shrugged. Sweat from the summer heat beaded on her mocha skin. The warm August air swelled with humidity, sticking to us, choking us. "I didn't see it happen, so you can't expect me to believe it was him."

"Fair enough."

We strolled through Cabildo Alley until we reached the broad side of St. Louis Cathedral. In front of us, a white sign on a black iron street lamp reminded us to be quiet in the church zone. We hooked a right and headed toward the Chartres Street plaza at the front end of the massive church.

An array of people filled the large slate courtyard that stretched as long as a city block. Small groups gathered near their tour guides at the steps of the church. A tired street vendor selling bottles of cold sodas and water took shelter from the sun under a red and white canopy. Passersby quickly glanced at the artwork laid against the iron fence that surrounded nearby Jackson Square. Charlatan fortune tellers settled at their folding tables willing to read palms for five dollars.

Elle and I sauntered through the plaza, taking in the menagerie.

"Camille, let me read a tarot card for you," a light-skinned, heavy-set woman shouted to us from her makeshift altar. Deep lines set in her face sagged beneath weathered eyes. Candles, cards, and a few trinkets spread out on the table in front of her. A weathered, hand-carved cane rested against the table.

Elle and I took a few more steps.

"Camille," the old woman called again. "I want to read your tarot card. Camille, come here."

Elle finally turned and acknowledged the aging woman when no other female in the area took notice of her.

"Are you talkin' to me?" Elle pointed to herself.

"Yes, Camille," the woman replied. She wore a long purple flowing dress, gold necklaces hung around her neck, and a black silk scarf wove through her white hair. "I have your tarot cards here."

"My name is Elle, not Camille," Elle insisted.

"You are Camille," the woman stood firm. "I know your story. You *and* your friend Will. He's not who he pretends to be."

I gasped. How did she know my name? Tension spread all over me. The sounds of the bustling crowd around me shrunk to a quiet hum. I couldn't concentrate on anything and felt like I was going to black out. My whole being wanted to shut down and escape into a puddle.

"What do you mean?" Elle said to the doddering woman, facing away from me.

"He knows who turned on the light in the wine cellar. He'll tell you soon enough, Camille."

Panic filled me like a cluster of igniting spark plugs inside me. My mind replayed what the woman said. How could she know my secret? The scorching August sun burned right through me. Thick humidity suffocated me. My stomach was in knots, like the last time I drank.

"Nice try," Elle replied, brushing off the woman. "My name is not Camille. I don't know how you know-- somebody must've told you-- but the cellar light was a faulty wire. Y'all have fun connin' the next person."

With her short legs, Elle scurried off down the plaza with me on her heels.

"Can you believe that joke of a woman? I should have told her off," Elle said to me as I approached a step behind her. Her annoyed eyes fixed on the flock of tourists ahead of us. "Why would she think my name is Camille? I get that the two names are close but come on. She wanted money to buy booze."

"I don't know," I robotically said, thankful that she couldn't see the anguished look of fear on my face.

CHAPTER 14

My Darling,   5 November, 1863

It has been six months since I left you in France and I miss you every single day. I am saving a lot of money to send for you. If everything goes as we planned, you will arrive here next summer. We can marry immediately. My heart longs for you.

Yours forever,
Frédéric

105

"Will! What are you doing?" Terrance found me the next morning on the storage room floor chucking knives into a large empty cardboard box like a street performer. A mound of silver steak knives piled beside me.

"Practicin' my knife throwin' act, what does it look like?" I sarcassed not turning to face him. My eyes shot forward without concentrating on anything. A sparkling knife left my hand with a whoosh and thudded into the cardboard. I picked up another one, clattering the pile of silver daggers next to me. Whoosh. Thud. Clatter. I grabbed another one. Whoosh. Thud. Clatter.

"I see that. But why are you throwin' knives?" Terrance stood hands on hips. "You're lucky that customers aren't allowed in here."

Ignoring his remark, I said, "Elle and I were at the plaza in front of the cathedral yesterday." Whoosh. Thud. Clatter.

"Yeah, and?"

"And..." I completed Terrance's sentence. Whoosh. Thud. Clatter. "We passed a street psychic."

"So what?" Terrance said. "Those people are con artists."

"Not this one," I replied. Whoosh. Thud. Clatter.

"What do you mean not this one?" Terrance studied me and raised an eyebrow. He stood still, concentrating on me.

"This street psychic called Elle *Camille*," I told him. Whoosh. Thud. Clatter.

"Oh," Terrance gasped, raising a hand to his mouth. "What'd she do?"

"You know Elle," I said. Whoosh. Thud. Clatter. "She blew it off like it was some kind of joke."

"That's good, right?" Terrance asked. Jutting, sparkling knives randomly decorated the cardboard box in front of him.

"Not really," I answered, still not facing Terrance. Whoosh. Thud. Clatter. "The street psychic recognized me and said my name. And she told Elle she knew who turned on the light in the wine cellar."

"What? How's that possible?" Terrance gasped again. "Did you talk to the woman first?"

"No," I stoically said. Whoosh. Thud. Clatter.

"What are you goin' to do?" he asked.

"I don't know. But this woman sounds like the real deal," I told him. Whoosh. Thud. Clatter. "I wish I drank now. I could use a stiff one."

"Let me know how I can help," Terrance told me. He turned and left me alone with my thoughts.

What was I going to do? Who was this mysterious fortune teller who called Elle Camille? I knew why she called Elle Camille, but how did this random woman figure it out? And how did she recognize me? How did she know my name? How did she know about the wine cellar light? I had never met her before nor told her anything about Elle. With deep wrinkles on her face and gypsy clothes, I would have remembered her if she came into the restaurant. Dizziness enveloped me from all of the unanswered questions running through me.

I had to find this woman again. I needed answers. Could she help me come up with a way to tell Elle how I knew her? What else did she know about me? And Elle? Did this woman always set up camp at the cathedral plaza or did she wander around the Quarter following the tourist lemmings?

Getting my bearings, I rose from the floor and yanked all of the knives out of the slaughtered cardboard box. I laid them in a plastic silverware crate and returned them to their proper place on the storage room shelf.

* * *

A few minutes later, I found Terrance setting tables in the main dining room. He glanced up at me with a look of anticipation.

"I gotta go do somethin'," I quickly told him. "I'll be back." Before Terrance could respond, I headed out the door.

Outside, I headed left out of Antoine's and half-jogged north on Royal Street, hastily dodging tourists and locals. A pony-tailed young man on a bike whizzed past me without pause. At the intersection of Toulouse and Royal, I wove my way around the Road Closed

108

barricades and several orange street safety cones. At the next block, I turned right on St. Peter Street. The narrow road maintained one single lane of one-way traffic in front of me. Trotting down St. Peter Street, I passed a homeless man sleeping in the alcove of The Arsenal museum.

At the corner of the next building, St. Peter Street met Chartres Street and the cathedral plaza opened up to me like the mouth of the Mississippi River. This was where Elle and I were the day before.

This early in the morning, the courtyard was sparsely filled. A few early-rising tourists snapped photos of the Jackson Square to the right of me. Two uniformed policemen strode through, patrolling their beat. Food street vendors opened up their carts offering Lucky Dogs and cold drinks. I searched for the fortune teller who called Elle Camille, but she was nowhere to be found. A pop-up band of a trumpeter, saxophonist, and drummer serenaded us with sounds of sweet jazz.

Another street psychic opened her umbrella and set up a folding table nearby.

Suddenly, the music stopped, and all was quiet around me. A chattering of pigeons on the sidewalk hushed.

"Excuse me," I said to the blonde woman. "Do you know all of the other fortune tellers around here?"

"Yes, we mostly know each other, if not by name, then by sight," she answered, spreading cards on her table.

"Yesterday, my friend and I came through here and encountered an older white woman who wore a long, purple dress and had a black scarf in her white hair," I told her. "Do you know who she is and where I can find her?"

"That's Madame Delia," the kind woman told me. "She moves around the Quarter every few days. She might not be back here until next week."

"Do you know where I could find her today?" I asked.

"No, I'm 'fraid I can't," the blonde woman said. "I stay in this plaza. You might want to try the other side of Jackson Square or on Bourbon."

"Thank you," my voice squeaked higher than usual. "You've been a great help!" I turned away before she could offer to read my palms.

The street musicians started playing again and the birds chirped in response.

I retraced my steps and headed back to St. Peter Street, with the fenced-in edge of Jackson Square on my left. I passed the antique shop where Elle bought the Coke sign for her auntie. Spicy aromatics of The New Orleans School of Cooking spilled onto the sidewalk. At the end of the block of the long, connected Pontalba shops, I made a left onto Decatur Street.

Artists displayed their colorful acrylics on the Jackson Square wrought iron fence. Mules tethered to 8-person carriages lined the street. City guides with IDs on a lanyard offered tours around the city on nearby parked buses. I rushed by many vendors on the sidewalk, but Madame Delia was nowhere to be found.

Making a left on St. Ann Street, I hoofed the three blocks to Bourbon Street. The street was fairly quiet this time of the morning. To my left, the seven hundred block brandished small bars and the rumored-to-be-haunted Bourbon Orleans Hotel. To my right, rainbow flags decorated several second-story iron galleries. I headed left, Fritzel's was further down the block. The yellow and green building was quiet now, promising live jazz music every night.

As I passed street psychics at their small tables, I kept my eye out for Madame Delia. I would never forget what she looked like. Again, she was nowhere to be found.

While most of the abutted buildings on the street were two or three stories, a one-story voodoo shop appeared out of place. The only window was shuttered closed. Intrigued and discouraged that I couldn't find Madame Delia, I wandered inside to be greeted by voodoo dolls, talismans, charms, and statues of local underworld gods and goddesses. Spicy incense filled the air. Eerie, ghostly music spooked the shop. A few curious tourists huddled in the corner debating whether to accept everything was real. I believed that a lot of New Orleans was haunted, but this paraphernalia seemed over the top.

The already-dim lights flickered off for a moment. The sinister music stopped.

Carefully, I approached a large, tattooed, and pierced shop clerk standing behind the counter. A black and red bandana encircled his bald head. He stared down at me, his dark eyes unmoving.

"Uh, hi," I stuttered, glancing around to see if anyone else could assist me. The large man frightened me. "Can you ... help me?"

He grunted.

"I'm lookin' for Madame Delia," I stated. "Do you know her?" I decided to keep my questions simple, fearing that any complexities might enrage the punk ogre who could have been a regular at One Eyed Jacks.

He glared at me sans blinking.

I lost the staring contest and, without an answer, turned to walk away.

"Preservation Hall," he grumbled.

Stopping in my tracks, I considered thanking the man for the information, but thought better of it and headed out the door.

CHAPTER 15

My Darling,   14 November, 1863

I toured Jackson Square today. Merchants and performers overflowed the large grassy area. Crowds gathered around watching a man juggling five glass bottles. The whole city is filled with a mixture of French, Spanish, Creole, Acadian, African, and Haitian people. I've never seen such a cosmopolitan destination. I anxiously await your arrival. I *miss you so much, ma chérie. You absorb me.*

Yours forever,
Frédéric

Despite its cult-like following for authentic jazz since the early 1960s, I almost missed Preservation Hall a couple of blocks away on St. Peter Street. The outside of the two-story building appeared as if someone had forgotten to paint it. Brown and green camouflage hues washed into the worn-out exterior. Closed ragged, wooden shutters prevented any sun from reaching the interior. The building was in sharp contrast to the adjoining well-maintained establishments. If I hadn't noticed the tiny sign hanging from the underside of the second-floor gallery stating `Preservation Hall`, I would have thought the building was abandoned. The property was quiet now, waiting in anticipation of nightly music.

Across the street, in front of Reverend Zombie's Voodoo Shop, Madame Delia settled into her folding-table-turned-fortune-telling stand. She was dressed the same as the last time I encountered her. Gold necklaces overlaid her long, flowy purple dress. A black silk scarf wrapped through her white hair. Gold hoop earrings reached her shoulders.

"Hello again, Will," she said to me, as I approached her.

"How do you know me? How do you know my name?" I demanded.

She studied me; a smug grin formed on her aged face. She silently picked up one of her tarot cards and pushed it, face down, to the edge of her table.

"Turn over the card," she instructed.

Nervous of what I was about to see, I gasped as I discreetly flipped it close to the surface of the table. The card depicted a naked Adam and Eve in front of God. Eve stood in front of the Tree of Knowledge. The title of the card was The Lovers.

"I know who you are," Madame Delia said to me. Her soft, old silver eyes examined me. "But do not worry, I will not tell Elle your secret."

A sigh of relief escaped my lips.

Madame Delia continued, "However, you need to tell her soon. Time is running out."

"What do you mean time is runnin' out? And how did you know about the light in the wine cellar?" I pressed.

"You already understand that Madame Delia knows things," she said.

Her refusal to give me straight answers frustrated me. I wanted to take my arm and swipe all of her tarot cards off the table and onto the sidewalk, but with several people walking nearby, I thought better of it. But Madame

Delia was right. She knew things. I gulped in a pocket of air.

"I will see you again soon, Will." She dismissed me with a slight wave of her hand and went back to studying the rest of her tarot cards.

I stomped away in defeat.

* * *

"Where have you been?" Elle reprimanded me, as I sauntered into Antoine's five minutes later. "You missed the lunch crowd and Terrance and I had to cover for you." She sat at one of the square tables in the large annex dining room, a stack of starched, white cloth squares in front of her. A pile of crisp, folded napkins was to her left.

"I went to get a wish granted by Marie Laveau," I lied. Urban legend dictated that if someone asked a wish of the 19th century voodoo queen and marked three Xs on her above-ground tomb in St. Louis Cemetery No. 1, the wish would come true. But lately, the cemetery had been under strict surveillance to prevent vandalism.

"Puh-lease." Elle rolled her eyes at me and turned back to folding napkins.

I wasn't ready to tell her the truth. Not yet. Madame Delia left me with many unanswered questions. I had to figure everything out first.

Elle spoke again, "While you were out wanderin' around town, Terrance and I made plans to meet up with his new *friend* at One Eyed Jacks. I think her name is

Rachel. If you want to come, we're goin' out after work tonight."

"Why did you say 'friend' like that?" I jested. "You jealous that Terrance has moved on after you turned him down?"

"Nooo," Elle denied through an obvious lie.

"If you say so." I chuckled and left Elle with her napkins.

* * *

Five hours later, Elle, Terrance, and I found ourselves amid the crowd at the entrance of One Eyed Jacks. Bald Rob perched on his bouncer's stool a few feet in front of us scrutinizing IDs.

"Elle, you'll want to pull out your ID," Terrance said. "Looks like Bald Rob is checkin' everyone. You were only in here once with us, so he might not remember you."

"Good idea." Elle pulled her wallet out of the small purse that hung from her shoulder.

We approached Bald Rob and he scanned Elle's license with his tiny blue flashlight.

He said to Terrance, "I know she's with you, but I still need to check. Alcohol and Tobacco Control is floatin' around tonight."

"No problem," Terrance said. "We know you're doin' your job."

"Have a good time," Bald Rob replied. "I'll catch up with you later after this crowd thins out."

"Thanks, bro," Terrance said, as we merged into the crowd at the inside entrance of the watering hole.

We maneuvered ourselves around other bar hoppers and stopped a few feet from the counter. Music blared at us from all angles.

"Do you see Rachel?" I asked Terrance.

"Not yet," he said, scanning the crowd. "I texted her earlier and she seemed excited to come tonight."

As we approached the packed red lacquered bar, the blue-haired bartender advanced toward us from the other side. Elle leaned into the bar as much as her short stature could allow. The crowd around us had lost any concept of personal space.

"I remember you," the bartender yelled to Elle over the music. "You're the neat Maker's Mark girl." She nodded in Terrance's direction. "I see you brought your girlfriend back too."

Elle barked a laugh and flicked a hand in Terrance's direction. "Yeah, but he's cool."

"You want Maker's Mark again tonight?" the bartender asked Elle.

"Yeah, that'd be great," Elle answered, holding up a pair of fingers. "Two."

The woman turned behind her to grab the bottle of amber libation on the shelf full of alcohol.

Terrance scoffed. "I've been in this place a hundred times and that bartender recognizes Elle after one night and doesn't remember me?"

"Aww, don't be jealous. Maybe you don't have the right parts?" Elle laughed, glancing down at her ample chest. "I'll make it up to you and buy the first round."

A minute later, the bartender set two short glasses of whisky on the counter in exchange for the twenty in Elle's hand.

Elle grabbed the glasses off of the bar, took a few steps, and handed one to Terrance. She clinked his glass with hers and swallowed half of the drink. He followed suit.

Suddenly, Elle jolted forward into Terrance's chest. He instinctively grabbed her with his free hand to prevent her from falling to the sticky floor.

"You okay?" he asked her, still holding her in his arm close to him. They locked eyes for a silent moment.

"Yes," she said, finally gazing away. "Some jerk knocked me from behind."

Terrance's gaze wandered down at her white t-shirt, his arm still hooked around her waist. "I didn't spill anything on you, did I?"

Elle followed his gaze down her chest. "Nah, I'm good."

Terrance finally released Elle and downed the rest of his drink.

I scanned the crowd, practicing my people-watching skills. A medley of bar hoppers encompassed us. A group of balding, golf-shirt-wearing, middle-aged men downed some beers to our left. Here for a convention. A girl in black leather shorts and a sliced-up Ramones t-shirt met her friends to our right. In the front lounge, the Island Snacks DJs filled the room with smooth jams.

Terrance followed my gaze.

"You lookin' for Rachel?" I asked him.

"Yeah, and I don't see her," he said.

"Maybe she texted you?" Elle interjected.

Terrance pulled his phone out of his pocket and grimaced as he read a text.

"What'd she say?" I asked him.

"She said she doesn't try out," Terrance replied, still absorbed in his phone.

"What does *that* mean?" Elle balked.

"It means," Terrance explained, and nodded to Elle. "Rachel was here and saw me drinkin' with you. And then she saw me huggin' you. She thinks you and I are on a date."

"That's BS. We aren't on a date and that wasn't a hug. It was because some idiot knocked me into you," Elle defended herself. "Where is she? I'll straighten it out."

"She's gone. She left," Terrance sighed.

"Her loss," Elle said and turned toward the bar. "Come on, I'll make it up to you and buy you another round."

Elle turned Terrance back to the bar and ordered two doubles of Maker's Mark from the blue-haired bartender.

Several drinks and lots of bantering later, Elle turned to me with glossy eyes. Those big, blue, beautiful eyes that mesmerized me. They complemented her soft, sultry voice. Oh, how I missed hearing that voice sing to me. I still wasn't sure how to tell Elle how I knew her. Madame Delia said time was running out, but I wasn't sure what that meant. Terrance stood fifteen feet away from us, studying the crowd.

"You don't drink, Will..." Elle said to me. "But do you dance?" She wiggled her hips in front of me, keeping in sync with the music.

"Nah, I can't. Two left feet," I said. "And I don't want to make you feel bad for dancin' with a poor idiot like me."

"Well then, I'll ask Terrance," Elle quipped, and she was off.

Out of the corner of my eye, I caught Terrance leaning into Elle with little space between them. He towered over her small stature. The music was so loud that he stepped closer to her to hear her asking him to dance. Or was it a convenient excuse to get closer to her?

A moment later, he trailed behind her to the middle of the dance floor, grazing his hand along the small of her back. They slipped into the crowd. With bottles raised, other clubbers surrounded them; bodies full of excessive energy. Almost every person in the place was dancing. wall-to-wall people bumped and grinded into each other.

I stood at the bar, watching. Elle danced inches away from Terrance, his arms jerking wildly above her. She cavorted next to him, her hips shifting back and forth with his. Elle danced in her own little world in front of Terrance. Even though I knew they were only friends, they appeared comfortable together. And, after all, Elle said she didn't date co-workers. I had nothing to worry about.

Elle reached up and wrapped her arms around Terrance's neck. He slipped his hands around her tiny waist and pulled her against him. My mouth fell open as they eliminated the platonic space between them. He moved her body back and forth with his, oblivious to me watching them. She faced him and smiled. He lifted her chin with the tips of his fingers.

Oh no, I knew what was coming. This was Terrance's move. I had seen him do it many times before. I tried in vain to fight my way through the crowd of people that separated me from them. But I was too late.

A couple of feet from them, I stopped in my tracks as Terrance passionately kissed Elle, his arms holding her tight.

How could he do this to me?

CHAPTER 16

My Darling,   24 November, 1863
Monsieur DuBois took me to Tujague's Restaurant tonight for dinner to celebrate his newest fleet acquisition. We ate a seven-course meal and learned the owners are from France. I wish you could have been there with me. You would have loved it. I cannot wait to marry you. You are the love of my life. You give me breath. You are my soul.
Yours forever,
Frédéric

The next morning, Elle found me sorting silverware at the servers' station. I didn't look up at her.

"Hi, Will," she said. "I have a new lead on the old picture. Wanna hear about it?"

The anger bubbling inside of me prevented me from being otherwise interested. I turned my shoulder to her as I placed a handful of spoons in the designated slot.

"Why don't you ask *Terrance*?" I snorted, without shifting my stance.

"Why would I ask T--" Elle didn't finish her sentence. "Oh, I get it. You think I lied about not datin' co-workers."

"I don't know," I sneered, finally facing her. "You tell me."

"Terrance and I are *not* dating!" Elle insisted. "So, we kissed. Big deal. Besides, you don't own me. I can do what I want. Why do you care anyway?"

"I'm glad you're so casual about all this," I scoffed.

"Will," Elle replied, her voice softening. "We got caught up in the moment. We were both drinkin' a lot. It just happened. I can assure you Terrance thinks the same thing. It's no big deal."

Even though I was mad about something that I conjured up in my mind, Elle's soulful cobalt eyes burned into me. The struggle between telling her how I knew her and preventing her from making Terrance feel like an idiot for kissing her because he had more than platonic feelings for her overwhelmed me. Until I figured everything out, helping my buddy won out. Even though I was just as angry at him. He and I were brothers from another mother.

"You'd better make sure Terrance thinks the same thing," I said, pursing my lips at her. "He's my best friend. Don't you hurt him."

"I promise you I won't. He's a good guy. I would never hurt him," Elle pleaded. Her soft features haunted me. "Do you want to hear about my new lead on the picture or not?"

"Yes," I conceded. I couldn't be mad at Elle for too long. It wasn't her fault that she didn't know my secret.

"Barney at Keil's called me this mornin' because he thought of somethin' else," Elle stated.

"What'd he say?" I wanted to know.

"He told me to talk to the owner at New Orleans Watchmakers on Carondelet Street," Elle said. "Barney said the guy knows everythin' about old pocket watches that have floated around the city over the years. Maybe I'll figure out who the man is in the picture if I start with the watch?"

"Maybe you will," I replied.

"And," Elle said, "since the shop is in the Central Business District, we'll have to take the streetcar."

"We?" I arched an eyebrow. "Do you have a mouse in your pocket?"

Elle chuckled. "I figured you'd want to come along since you've kept me company every other time."

"I'm messin' with ya," I said through a smile. Even though streetcars were a challenge for me, I'd have to get over my fear for Elle. Ironically, Terrance took a streetcar to work every day and I avoided them like the plague. "Of course, I'll come. When are we goin'?"

"Our next day off," Elle replied.

"Sounds good to me," I said and quietly inhaled.

* * *

After the last party of the lunch crowd left the main dining room, I cleared off the dirty tablecloth, bundled it and the dirty napkins in my hands, and headed down the hall toward the linen room. Terrance emerged from the Large Annex Room and was on my heels.

"Hey man." He reached his arm toward me. "Where've you been all day? I barely saw you durin' the lunch rush."

"Around." I avoided Terrance's eyes. He knew my secret and how I knew Elle. His betrayal burned me. Elle's ignorance was her excuse. Terrance didn't have that same luxury.

"Oh, I get it," he said. "You're mad about last night."

"What the hell, man!" I bellowed so loud that the petite chandelier on the ceiling above us rattled.

"I told you who Elle is, and you go and kiss her!" I roared.

"Will, chill," Terrance softly pleaded, spreading the fingers of his hands toward me.

"How could you do this to me?" My voice turned into a deep growl and my eyes stabbed into him like daggers. "I thought we were friends! Brothers!"

"I'm sorry, Will," Terrance sighed. "I didn't plan on kissin' her. It just happened. I swear. We good?"

His apology seemed sincere, but I was still vexed.

"God, y'all are so casual about this," I huffed. "Doesn't anyone believe in love or real relationships anymore?"

"Yes, I do," Terrance answered. "I envy your constant faith and hope in love. More people should be like *you*. Charles told me what you did for those two people in the bar. He said they came back together a few days later and he saw them kissin'."

Terrance's kind words soothed me. He and I had been friends for a long time, and this was the first time we fought over a girl. I hated fighting with him. We were tight.

"But I still don't want you to have Elle," I protested.

"Will. Come on." Terrance focused his dark eyes on me and his voice took a serious tone. "You know you can't have her. It's *not* possible."

CHAPTER 17

My Darling,   1 December, 1863

I know how much you love pralines. You cannot get enough of those sugared almonds. But the candies are a little different here in Vieux Carré than in France. Since almonds are not readily available, the local French substitute pecans instead and add cream. The street sellers sing "Soeur Rosalie au retour de matines, Plus d'une fois lui porta, des pralines." They are as tasty as the ones I used to eat with you. I *am sure you will love them as much as I love you. You are sweet, like a praline.*

Yours forever,
Frédéric

On our next day off a few days later, I met Elle in front of Jean Lafitte's Old Absinthe House at the corner of Bourbon and Bienville Streets. Local legend recounted that the 300-year-old building was the meeting place for General Andrew Jackson and the infamous New Orleans pirate, Jean Lafitte, during the War of 1812. Jackson agreed to release Lafitte's band of misfits from prison and grant full pardons to any of them who would fight alongside him in the Battle of New Orleans.

Elle wiped the sweat from her forehead as a fog of humidity suffocated us. "One of these years, I need to take a month-long vacation somewhere cooler. This heat is brutal. Even in the mornin'." The canvas bag holding the antique photo hung from her shoulder.

"Yeah," I said. "But you'll be happy where you live come January when everyone else is under a foot of snow up north."

I motioned to the white building behind me. Red and white umbrellas shaded bistro dining tables on the second-story gallery.

"You know," I said, "this place is haunted too."

Elle rolled her eyes. "You won't give up on this, will you?"

"But it's true," I said. "Jean Lafitte, in his signature pirate hat, throws the occasional ghost party and is blamed for unexplained ruckus and carousing inside after the living party goers have gone home."

"That place is full of drunk tourists who buy that crap," Elle scoffed and gazed over my shoulder.

I turned my head and followed her line of sight through the tall, green first-floor open doors. She was right; the dark inside was already filled with intoxicated patrons overflowing the copper bar.

"Come on," Elle directed me back to the street. "We have a watch to find."

As much as I loved the Quarter, I avoided this section of Bourbon Street as much as possible. Most buildings in front of us displayed pink and green neon signs advertising half-naked showgirls, voodoo charlatans, and big-ass beers. The overpowering stench of urine made me nauseous. This time of day, most of the drunk devotees were inside. After seven o'clock, this section of the street would be wall-to-wall people searching for watered-down drinks and half-dressed dancers. Most of the buildings in this block didn't display any flags or extra decorations like other parts of the Quarter, because they would be stolen or destroyed by inebriated-fueled debauchery.

This morning, a handful of construction workers in chartreuse vests and white hard hats gathered at the end of a backhoe digging a hole in the street. One of them ogled Elle a little longer than I was comfortable.

"Did you see that guy checkin' you out?" I asked her, a few steps later.

"Yeah," she answered. "But he's harmless. It's the ones who corner me who I have to threaten their ability to make babies with a well-placed knee."

I barked a laugh.

I admired Elle's fortitude. She accepted that she garnered unwanted attention with her curvy, petite frame and exotic looks but she knew how to fight off the hungry dogs.

We crossed Iberville Street, the Hard Rock Café on our right, and Bourbon House Seafood on our left. A few utility trucks took up most of the space on the narrow street.

In a dozen more strides, we reached the starting point of Bourbon Street, the upriver end of the Quarter. With Canal Street in front of us, I paused at the St. Charles Avenue Streetcar stop on the corner. I inhaled deeply, mentally preparing myself for the ancient wooden trolley ride.

"What are you doin'?" Elle asked.

"Waitin' for the streetcar," I answered. "You said we had to take it."

"Actually, we don't," Elle explained. "When I Googled the watch shop, it was on the first block of Carondelet." She pointed across Canal Street to our destination. The original avenue had plans to be a water canal that never came to fruition.

I exhaled loudly.

"What's that about?" Elle asked.

"I don't do streetcars," I said.

Elle tried to stifle a laugh. "What do you mean you don't do streetcars? You don't ride them? They're pretty harmless, you know. It's not like they go 100 miles an hour. I bet I could bike faster."

I stared at the sidewalk, avoiding her.

Elle stopped laughing at me. "It's okay, I get it. Some people are afraid of heights, you're afraid of streetcars."

"Yeah, somethin' like that," I replied.

We waited for the light, crossed Canal Street, and headed down Carondelet. Stale grey buildings stretched in front of us. The quiet, monotone Central Business District paled in comparison to the lively, multi-colored French

Quarter behind us. We passed a sign for the NOLA Downtown Music and Arts Festival.

Elle stopped in front of an ash-colored building, studying tall, black iron gates before her. No marquee advertised what was inside. The adjacent onyx awning covered tall sheets of particle board that protected a broken window.

"Is this it?" I asked her.

"I think so," she said, pushing open the iron gate.

In the vestibule to our right, we found an interior door touting `New Orleans Watchmakers` on the window. A glass etching of a gold Rolex accompanied the words.

Elle opened the door and we headed into a shop lined with glass display cases filled with Tag Heuer, Bulova, Breitling, and Cartier timepieces. Stark fluorescent lights illuminated the room. A middle-aged man in a grey golf shirt and black trousers looked up from the gutted watch in front of him. Several clocks with different times hung on the wall behind him.

"Hello," he said to Elle.

"Hi," she said to him. "I was wonderin' if you could help me."

"Hopefully," he said, with a warm smile. "What can I do for you?"

"Do you know anythin' about old watches?" Elle asked him.

"You've come to the right place. I recently restored a 1952 Rolex," he replied.

Elle pursed her lips. "How about somethin' older than that? Like from the 1860s."

"Oh, you mean like this?" The man pointed to the antique marble and bronze table clock next to him resting atop the glass display case.

"Yes," Elle said, pulling the antique photo from the bag on her shoulder. "I know you can't see much of it in this picture, but I was wonderin' if you ever get any leads on old pocket watches."

"Hmmm..." the man pondered and reached for the photo with an open palm. "May I?"

"Yes, of course," Elle replied and handed him the picture frame.

He pulled a tiny magnifying scope out of his shirt pocket, pressed it to his eye, and examined the photo.

"Can you see the details of the pocket watch with that?" Elle questioned him.

"Unfortunately, no," he said, still scrutinizing the man in the picture. "But I was trying to see if I could tell if this gentleman could give me any kind of clue." He finally gazed at Elle. "It will be tough though."

Elle huffed a sigh of disappointment.

"Let me look into this and call some of my contacts. Maybe they know something that I don't," the man told her.

"Give me your name and number and I'll give you a call if I find out anything."

I waited as Elle gave the man her contact information.

Five minutes later, we waited at the corner of Carondelet and Canal Streets. A steady stream of blaring cars, taxis, and buses crossed in front of us.

"That was a total bust," Elle groaned.

"Maybe not," I said, attempting to raise her spirits. "Maybe that guy can come up with somethin'." I wanted to add *just be careful what you wish for*.

For a quick moment, Elle stared at me with those mesmerizing, cyan eyes. Soon enough, she would discover who the man in the photo was.

Even though she didn't find out anything new about the antique photo, the slight smile on Elle's face made her appear content. As I spent more time with her, I learned her humor and strong personality made her an amazing woman. In the end, Terrance would have to fight me for her. I quietly chuckled knowing duels were outlawed these days.

Then I remembered his prophecy. Even if I have to perform some unconventional favors to the underworld and sell my soul to Marie Laveau, I would make Elle mine.

CHAPTER 18

My Darling,   9 December, 1863

Last night, I was up late and could not sleep. With the moon and oil street lamps guiding me, I went for a stroll and ended up on the other side of the Cathedral. I found Café du Monde at the French Market. Fortunately, it is open all night for those times I am up thinking of you. I was so intrigued by the market last night, I went back again this morning before work. The complex houses Halles des Bouchéries (like

my name, soon to be yours) and
Halles des Legumes. Servants and
housewives were out with their
kitchen baskets, mingling with fur
traders, peddlers, buccaneers, and
bargemen. I stopped at the linen
peddler and bought us a beautiful
ivory silk tablecloth for our dining
table. I cannot wait for you to see
it. I miss you so much, ma chérie.

Yours forever,
Frédéric

A few mornings later, the lunch staff congregated in the kitchen surrounding Chef Miguel, anxiously waiting to hear about the day's specials. A dozen stainless steel pots and pans hung from an overhead rack above his head. Stalks of celery and scallions lay in wait on silver trays, ready to be diced up for stock.

"Today's summer lunch special starts with a choice of three appetizers," Chef Miguel told us. "Local charbroiled oysters are still in season, so we'll have them for a while. We also have vichyssoise to chill our guests from the heat." He pulled a clean rag from his chef coat breast pocket and wiped a trickle of sweat from his forehead. "And we have a spring green salad filled with baby spinach, plump strawberries, and shaved carrots. It's tossed with pepper jelly vinaigrette. Mmm... one of my favorites."

"I think all of Chef's dishes are 'one of his favorites'," I chuckled to Terrance in the back of the crowd.

Chef Miguel ignored my light-hearted heckle. "As for the entrees, we have grilled drum. The fisherman told me he caught it himself along the oyster reef this mornin'. It has a side of Florentine rice and is topped with a beurre blanc sauce." The entire wait staff scribbled furiously as he spoke. "As another seafood option, we're servin' scallop étouffée with peas over steamed white rice. The last entree option is fried chicken breast covered in a marmalade drizzle with three-cheese macaroni and collard greens."

"Mmm...mmm... reminds me of home," Elle spoke loud enough for Terrance and me to hear her. "My mama makes the best collard greens."

"What's for dessert today, Chef?" I yelled from the back of the crowd.

"Glad you could join us today, Will," Chef Miguel jested, taking a jab at my unexplained absence the previous week. "Our desserts today are creamy cheesecake with caramel sauce and dark chocolate mousse topped with whipped cream."

"I'll make sure Terrance stays away from the cheesecake," I quipped, in a feeble attempt to show off in front of Elle. "His uniform is tight."

Terrance dropped his jaw faking insult then smiled broadly, knowing I outed his penchant for the delicious dessert.

"Have a great day everyone. And don't forget," Chef Miguel, spoke above the dispersing crowd. "The mayor and her staff are comin' next week for lunch. We need to be better than perfect."

I followed Terrance and Elle out of the kitchen and into the main dining to finish setting up for the lunch crowd. I grabbed clean water carafes from the shelf to fill them.

"Are you guys goin' to One Eyed Jacks this weekend?" Elle asked us.

"Probably," Terrance replied. "Why?"

"Well…" Elle explained, "if you're up for a change of pace, my daddy's band is playin' at The Spotted Cat on Saturday night if you want to see them. And my sister is singin'."

"Sure, I'd love to," Terrance said. "Sounds fun."

"Me too," I added.

"Do we need tickets?" Terrance asked.

"No," Elle said. "There's no cover charge. They play at 10:00 so we'll have to rush out of here right after we're done with work. Bring cash because they don't take plastic."

"That's not a problem for us," Terrance laughed, referring to the unspoken benefit of being a restaurant server. "And if there are any stragglers at dinner, I'll see if I can pawn them off on Georgia."

"Or I can always see if I can push them along." I winked at Terrance. "Elle, does your dad know you asked us to come?"

"Yes," she said. "He said he can't wait to meet y'all."

"Lookin' forward to it," I replied. I couldn't wait to meet Elle's dad. Maybe he could indirectly give me some clues on how to tell Elle that I knew her?

We finished setting up for lunch with fifteen minutes to spare before the first group of diners wandered in seeking solace from the stifling summer humidity.

* * *

On Saturday night, as Terrance predicted, one last table of four lingered in his section of the Large Annex Room.

He anxiously checked his watch from behind the dining room door. "It's 9:15 and these people got their bill 15 minutes ago and have yet to pay it." Terrance huffed in exasperation. "If they don't leave soon, we will miss Elle's dad. And Georgia already left so I can't give them to her." Elle's last table had packed up twenty minutes earlier and she waited for us in the kitchen noshing on leftover chocolate mousse.

I peered out through the swinging door's window. "What do you want me to do?"

"I don't know, man," Terrance replied. "Think of somethin'."

The leisurely party in the dining room consisted of two couples in their early 50s. They were old enough to afford a bottle of Gould Campbell 1975 but young enough to appreciate it. I watched from the dining room door window as the dark-haired man poured the remaining vintage port from the bottle into his companion's glasses and set the empty bottle near the edge of the table. The blonde woman next to him raised her glass in salute and took a long sip. Her friends did the same.

I glanced around the otherwise-empty dining room. All of the other tables were cleared and reset with a clean, crisp tablecloth ready for the next day. The brass chandeliers hanging from the ceiling were dimmed to a soft haze. The light sconces on the walls provided the remaining illumination in the red and chestnut room.

"I have an idea," I told Terrance, pushing through the swinging door. "I'm apologizin' in advance, but hopefully it will get us out of here soon."

I inched along the perimeter of the room and sauntered up to the remaining table. The couples continued talking and didn't notice me. With a swift motion,

I hooked my finger around the top of the empty port bottle. The bottle tipped toward the floor and I stepped away as fast as I could.

The loud crash caused the companions to jump from their seats to get away from the broken glass. The dark-haired man spoke, "Is everyone okay? I could have sworn I put that bottle far enough away from the edge."

His friends double-checked themselves for stray glass and confirmed they were unharmed.

Terrance bolted from the dining room door and made a beeline for his table.

"I'm so sorry," he professed, making sure his patrons were not harmed by any broken glass. "I'll get that cleaned up right away."

"Maybe it's time for us to head out anyway," the blonde woman said. She lifted her wine glass from the table, raised it to her mouth, and drained the remaining port. Her friends followed suit.

"Let me pay the bill while you're here," the dark-haired man said to Terrance as he retrieved his wallet from his jacket pocket. He slid out a credit card and placed it in the small black folder that had been sitting on the table for fifteen minutes.

Terrance took the bill folder from the man and headed toward the kitchen. I was on his heels.

"That was risky, Will," Terrance told me. "But it worked. You're one lucky bastard."

CHAPTER 19

My Darling,   *21 December, 1863*

I know I should be saving money to send for you, but I could not help myself today. One of the jewelry vendors at the French Market displayed an Old Mine Cut Diamond necklace. I splurged and bought it for you for a Réveillon de Noël present even though I will not see you for the holiday. The necklace has five pendants set in gold and topped with silver. It will look lovely around your beautiful neck.

144

I would love for you to wear it on our wedding day. I will never stop loving you.
    Yours forever,
    Frédéric

Fifteen minutes after Terrance and I cleaned up the broken wine bottle, we met Elle on the sidewalk outside of Antoine's. Terrance wore relaxed jeans and a grey V-neck t-shirt. Elle donned a blue and magenta bohemian striped sundress and a jean jacket. They made a striking couple standing next to each other. I hated it.

"If you two don't mind walkin' down Royal for about a mile," Elle said, "it's easier than waitin' for the streetcar on Decatur."

I shot her a nervous glance.

"Oh, right," Elle said. "For whatever reason, Will doesn't do streetcars anyway. One of these days you'll have to tell me why you're so afraid of them."

"I'm not givin' away all my secrets," I jested with a smile. "Not yet, at least."

Elle brushed me off with a laugh. "Once we get past Governor Nicholls Street, it gets a little shady. I'm glad you two are with me this time of night."

"Don't worry. We would never let anythin' happen to you," Terrance replied as he slid his arm around Elle's shoulders. I could have sworn he ogled her for an extra second.

We made a left away from Antoine's and rounded the first corner then made a left onto Royal Street in front of the Maison Royale jewelry gallery. A garland of giant purple, gold, and green balls hung from the second-story iron gallery. A complementary white Mardi Gras mask guarded the night like a mystical figurehead on the bow of a ship.

We headed down Royal, weaving our way around the nocturnal crowds who had no patience for the drunk tourists on Bourbon Street a block away. The black streetlamps guided our way along the narrow, grey sidewalk. Most of the antique galleries and boutiques had closed their doors hours ago, but adjoining restaurants were filled with twilight patrons.

As we crossed St. Peter Street two blocks later, the lights of St. Louis Cathedral illuminated the sky on our right.

"Look," Terrance said, pointing to the large shadow cast on the back wall of the massive church. "It's Touchdown Jesus."

Behind the cathedral, St. Anthony's Garden was once a popular place for duels near the local priest to give last rights to the loser. These days, the quiet, serene garden was fenced off to tourists and vagrants. The grassy courtyard still housed a few statues and monuments, the tallest being a cement obelisk. A few yards away, and half the size, an unobtrusive Tuscan marble statue of Jesus raised his hands in praise. During Hurricane Katrina, the figure lost a forefinger and a thumb.

Now, after the sun went down and a forward-thinking electrician purposely directed some spotlights, it was evident how the statue earned its moniker. The shadow of the effigy almost reached the roof of the colossal French Neo-Gothic church and could be seen from the next block.

"You know that's how the Saints won the Super Bowl in 2010, right?" I added. "Touchdown Jesus helped them."

"Oh, please." Elle rolled her eyes. Those deep eyes that captivated me. "You two and your local legends..."

"It's true," Terrance laughed with a wide smile, grazing Elle's arm.

"I wouldn't lie to you," I said.

We crossed St. Ann and Dumaine Streets, slowly easing our way into the residential section of the Quarter. A few cafés and boutique hotels nestled between pastel homes decorated with low-hanging ferns and multicolored fleur de lis banners. We passed the brightly lit Cornstalk Hotel that earned its name from the 19th century black iron fence forged in the shape of corn stalks in the front yard.

At the corner of Royal and Governor Nicholls Streets, a sudden chill overcame me, and I shuddered.

"Will, you okay?" Elle asked as we stopped on the sidewalk. Terrance shot me a look of concern.

"I don't know," I replied. "I think so. It was weird. Like someone pushed me."

"My hands were in my pockets, I swear!" Terrance jested. "If anythin', I'd brush up against Elle. She's hotter than you."

Elle barked a laugh.

I glanced upward at the grey three-story building hovering above us. Next to a black double door, a white and blue tiled mosaic placard on the side of the building read: When New Orleans was the Capital of the Spanish Province of Louisiana 1762-1803 This street bore the name Calle Real.

"Look where we are," my voice cracked with concern.

Terrance and Elle stepped off the sidewalk, into the empty street and inspected the old mansion. A black iron fence wrapped around the second story forming a large balcony. A couple of the windows lit up from the inside, but otherwise, the place was dark.

"No idea," Elle huffed. "It's too dark to see much. Where are we?"

"The LaLaurie Mansion," Terrance replied. "This buildin' is the most haunted house in New Orleans. Slaves were tortured here for years. A friend of mine went in one night and came back with scratches down his back. It's a private residence now, but tours used to be able to go inside."

"And gawk," Elle finished his sentence. "I hear about this place around every Halloween where people claim to see and hear all sorts of weird things. But I never paid attention to where it was." She and Terrance rejoined me on the sidewalk.

"But somethin' pushed me," I pressed. "I know it."

"You sure you didn't trip?" Elle joked.

"Positive," I said.

She shook her head at me in disbelief.

I knew what I felt. I glanced around as we walked away, making sure no one, or nothing, was following us.

We sauntered down Royal Street as minuscule front yards and small trees separated the homes from the sidewalk, unlike the commercial section of the Quarter where the sidewalk abutted the buildings.

After we crossed Esplanade Avenue, Elle paused in front of a house on the 1400 block of Royal Street. Sparse streetlamps dimly lit the road as a few people meandered on the opposite sidewalk.

"Look at this house," she said, pointing to a newly renovated, red brick, long and narrow camelback home.

"It's so out of place next to this older white and blue shotgun house. I mean it has a garage and everything. No one has an attached garage in the Quarter. And who has a brick house around here?" She stepped a few feet away from Terrance and me to marvel at the modern home.

"Maybe the original house was damaged in Katrina and it had to be demolished?" Terrance guessed.

I stopped and blinked in disbelief. "Oh my god," I whispered to myself.

Terrance heard me and said, "What? What's wrong, man?"

"I used to live here," I spoke quietly so that Elle couldn't hear me. The exterior of the house had been updated, but the block was the same. I remembered magnolia trees and orchids in adjoining back gardens, jazz music echoing out of my neighbors' windows, and the aroma of hush puppies being baked in kitchens. Beyond the inky shadows over the roof, I could still see a massive oak tree in the back that once provided me shade. When I lived here, I had so many hopes and dreams.

"The house is different now," I whispered to Terrance, "but it's the same place. You *can't* tell her."

CHAPTER 20

My Darling,   31 December, 1863
    Thank you for the bronze inkwell for my Réveillon de Noël gift. I will think of you even more every time I write you a letter. How is that possible when you are always in my thoughts? On Christmas Eve, Monsieur DuBois invited me to his home for a feast of seafood gumbo, roast meats, dressings, desserts, eggnog, and wine. His family is repeating it tonight. I wish you were with me to celebrate. I think of

nothing else until I can kiss your tender lips again. You fill me with love and make my life whole. I cannot wait for you to get here so that we can spend the rest of our lives together. You have a way of making me feel loved like I have not known before. When I write you again, the New Year will have started, and it will be the beginning of a delightful year for us.

Yours forever,
Frédéric

Five minutes later, the three of us made a right on Frenchman Street in the Marigny. The offbeat district had a reputation for Cajun bistros, intimate jazz clubs, and bohemian bars. Multi-colored strands of leftover Mardi Gras beads hung from the trees above us. On the block ahead, a 20ish man in a gray fedora serenaded us with his trumpet.

A small crowd formed in front of the second building on the left. Gold letters touting The Spotted Cat Music Club were inscribed on the top of the wooden

152

double-door frame. A red neon OPEN sign welcomed us. Large green framed windows hugged the doorway vestibule. To the right, the metal gate to the Frenchman Art Market cement courtyard was locked for the night.

Elle led the way as we joined the flock of people waiting to get in. Ahead of us on the right, a bouncer in a black t-shirt and jeans checked IDs. I skirted to the left side of Terrance and Elle to avoid bumping into the woman in line in front of me.

"IDs please," the bored bouncer said to Terrance and Elle, his palm upright waiting for them to hand their licenses to him. They obliged and pulled their IDs out to be verified.

"He missed you," Elle said to me as we made our way inside.

"Guess he didn't see me," I told her, and she turned toward the inside of the club.

Terrance quietly scoffed and threw me a side glance. Behind Elle's back, I raised an index finger to my lips to silently hush Terrance.

"Let's go," Elle said to us, without turning around. "I see my daddy." She reached her hand back to lead us through the crowd and Terrance snatched it up.

In a few steps, I followed Elle and Terrance into the cozy club. Above us, a colorful shop-front sign declared the one drink minimum per set rule. On the other side of a wooden handrail, a hodgepodge of old dining room chairs sat empty waiting for Elle's dad's band to get settled and start playing. A double bass rested against a stand near the windows. An upright piano sat silent along the wall in front of the small stage with a sign above it that warned No Drinks on the Piano. On the far green wall, a cartoon silhouette of a beatnik cat played a saxophone. Jazz and blues aficionados filled the intimate space. Overhead, music from the native Marsalis royal family entertained us through sound speakers until the live performers were ready to sing.

Elle led us through the crowd to the far end of the bar, near the back of the room. She stopped at an older, dark-skinned man with close-cropped black hair sitting in the last barstool. The shape of his eyes was the same as Elle's, but the color was different.

He wore a white button-down shirt and grey slacks. A blue tie with tiny white polka dots wrapped loosely around his neck below the unbuttoned collar of his shirt. A trumpet rested quietly in his lap. He seemed confident and relaxed as if performing gave a jolt of energy to his maturing body.

"Daddy!" Elle's face brought on new vigor that I had never seen before.

The man got up and embraced Elle, practically swallowing her tiny body whole in his arms.

"Hi, Sugar," he said to his daughter. "Your sister is up front minglin'. Did you see her?"

"Yes, I did," Elle replied after he released her. "But I didn't get a chance to talk to her. The place is packed. Daddy, these are my friends." She pointed to us. "Terrance and…"

Suddenly, the lights in the room flickered and the overhead music stopped playing. The few people nearby surveyed the room figuring out the unexpected change in scene.

"That was weird," Elle's dad said, his eyes scrutinizing his surroundings. "Maybe we have a ghost?" He barked a laugh at his joke.

Elle chuckled in response and then turned her attention to me. "Daddy, this is Will."

"Good to meet y'all," he said to Terrance and me, with a broad smile full of radiant teeth contrasting against his dark skin. "Please call me Sam."

"Nice to meet you, Sam," Terrance said.

"Good to meet you, Sam," I repeated.

"Elle tells me you helped find a birthday present for my sister Viola," Sam said to me.

"Yes, sir, I did," I said.

"Thank you for doin' that." He beamed at me. "She's a tough old broad to buy for."

"Daddy!" Elle warned.

Sam gestured to the empty musician chairs at the front of the room. "Well, we're gettin' started soon if y'all want to take a seat."

155

Elle, Terrance, and I hung back at the bar while Sam made his way through the standing-room-only crowd and stepped up onto the small stage at the front.

He spoke into a microphone stand, "How y'all doin' tonight?"

The audience cheered and whistled at him.

"So glad y'all could come tonight. Y'all ready for some jazz and blues?" Sam said. As he spoke, three men and a woman joined him on stage with instruments in their hands settling into the wooden chairs. "We're the Craw Daddy Jazz Band and we'll be entertainin' y'all for the next coupla hours." More cheers and whistles from the packed audience.

Sam spoke again, "We have a special treat for y'all tonight. My daughter Nina is singin' with us. She's been performin' in Biloxi for the past coupla years and has come back home to N'Awlinz."

The room erupted in applause.

Through the accolades, a young woman in her late 20s made her way around the crowd at the front of the room. She wore a snug black strapless dress that accentuated her curves. Taller than Elle, Nina had her sister's cocoa skin and long, dark, wavy hair. As she took the stage, the musicians behind her lifted their brass instruments. One of the men hugged the double bass.

"Your sister is hot," Terrance pointed out to Elle.

"Don't get any ideas," Elle retorted with a side-eye.

"Believe me, I know what I want," Terrance told her, loud enough for me to hear.

I glared in his direction.

The overhead lights dimmed, and a spotlight shined on Nina.

An hour later, after listening to Nina sing songs by Otis Redding, Aretha Franklin, and a few other greats, the house lights turned on to signal a set break.

Sam and Nina stepped off the stage and headed toward us. A 30ish dark-skinned man set his trombone down on his chair and followed them.

The three of them approached us at the back of the bar. Empty glasses of Maker's Mark rested on the counter in front of Elle and Terrance.

"Will and Terrance," Elle said, gesturing to the younger man. "This is my brother Nat and my sister Nina."

"Good to meet y'all," Nat said to us. His blue eyes twinkled like his sister's.

"He doesn't have the voice his sisters have," Sam interjected, "but he can play a mean trombone."

"Daddy, you know I don't like to sing in front of people." Elle blushed sheepishly. Something I hadn't seen her do since I caught her singing.

"Sugar, you sing as good as Nina," Sam reassured her. "I don't know why you think otherwise."

"It's true," I added. Nina possessed a velvety voice, but it didn't mesmerize me the way Elle's did. "I heard her.

She's amazing. She was singin' in the wine cellar at work one day. Her voice brought me back to another time." That voice. That voice that used to calm me on my darkest days.

"Elle, why don't you sing tonight?" Nina suggested. "I can take a break."

"I can't...I can't..." Elle sighed.

"Yes. You can," Terrance urged, sliding an arm around her shoulders. "Focus on me and don't worry about anyone else. Watch me. I'll help you. I promise you you'll be okay."

A jolt of jealousy simmered inside me as Terrance concentrated on Elle. She seemed comfortable with his discreet affection toward her in front of her family. He had been casually flirting with her all night and it tore me up. I couldn't yet tell Elle how I knew her and how I felt about her. I still had to figure that out. But I didn't want Terrance taking away my opportunity.

"Sugar, you can do it," Sam pressed, gesturing to himself and his son. "I'll be right there with you. Nat will be too."

"Okay, okay," Elle succumbed to our gentle persuasion. "I'll do it."

Ten minutes later, Sam, Nat, and Elle made their way to the stage. Again, Sam stepped up to the microphone. Elle waited next to him, nervously curling the hem of her dress in her fingers.

158

"We have a slight change of plans tonight," he spoke to the audience. "My *other* daughter, Elle, will be singing a few songs for us tonight. She's a little shy, so let's give her a big warm welcome to The Spotted Cat."

Along with Sam, the crowd hollered and applauded. Nina, Terrance, and I cheered from the back. Terrance raised his fingers to his mouth and blew out a loud whistle. His face beamed at Elle. I could tell he was falling for her.

Sam took a seat behind Elle and lifted his trumpet. The overhead lights dimmed again and a spotlight shined on her. She took a deep breath and stepped closer to the microphone. Elle glanced back toward her dad and took another breath. Her blue eyes locked on Terrance sitting next to me.

She serenaded us with the snap-worthy tune "Fever."

That voice... What was I going to do? I had to figure it out soon.

CHAPTER 21

My Darling,   10 January, 1864
The War of Northern Aggression still rages around me. Les Americains call it that. I try to stay out of it because I don't understand it. It is difficult to walk the streets some days and not see the military takeover and the toll the war has on the locals even though most of the battles are much farther north. I pray that when you get here, the city will be calmer, and we can live our life in harmonie. I

want you and our future children to see the beauty of Vieux Carré as I do. I cannot wait to share everything about this magnificent city with you.

Yours forever,
Frédéric

The next morning, I escaped to the second-floor gallery of Antoine's to gather my thoughts while the rest of my coworkers prepped for the lunch crowd. My arms draped on the rail. In front of me, green, yellow, and purple banners flapped in a cool breeze, relieving the oppressive August humidity. A few people walked on the sidewalk below, not noticing me. Potted plants hung from the gallery roof above me.

My thoughts wandered to Elle. The more time I spent with her, the more I was convinced that I had known her in another life. Her eyes, her voice, her spunk, the way she made me laugh. I remembered falling in love with her before. But yet, she treated me like a friend or a brother. She didn't know who she was. I needed to tell her. Convincing her wouldn't be easy.

Seeing Elle with her dad and siblings made my heart melt. Their love and respect for each other could set the bar for drama-filled families. I remembered having a family like that. I would have done anything for them. Elle's family made me want to be with her even more.

What about Terrance? He was my best friend; I could tell him anything. He and I shared a powerful bond. But I remembered the way he gazed at Elle. Even though he brushed off their kiss, I knew he was falling for her. She seemed to reciprocate, especially after staring at him while she sang last night. He helped calm her, something I had not done. She sang directly to him last night.

My secret prevented me from telling Elle who I was. But if I wanted to have a future with her, she deserved to know the truth. If I told her, she and I might find a way to be together. Unfortunately, I had no idea how she would react. She might not believe me. She might laugh at me. She might call me a liar. She might never speak to me again. I couldn't bear that.

Nor did I want to hurt Terrance.

Who could help me tell Elle the truth and win her heart at the same time without hurting Terrance?

I stood up straight with an idea, accidentally knocking an overhead potted fern from its hook and sending it crashing to the sidewalk below.

The ceramic-bowled plant narrowly missed a couple standing on the sidewalk, shattering in front of them. The man made sure his female companion was unharmed and they both looked up to the gallery where I stood. I slid inside the second-floor doors, cursing myself for the careless thing I did. I prided myself on being cautious.

"What the heck?" the man muttered from below. "How did a plant fall down here on its own?"

"Maybe the chain snapped?" the woman pondered.

"That's so weird," the man said. "I don't see anything up there."

Five minutes later, I found Terrance in the kitchen talking to Chef Miguel. The kitchen staff scurried around them planning the daily lunch specials.

"I need to go do somethin'," I told them. "I'll be back."

Before they could respond, I vanished from the kitchen.

* * *

Outside, I hoofed the two blocks north to St. Peter Street and stopped in front of Preservation Hall. A handful of people wandered down the street. A morning delivery van parked in front of a cigar shop. A woman in a long sundress rested against the exterior wall of Pat O'Brien's restaurant, talking on her phone and smoking a cigarette.

The sidewalk in front of Reverend Zombie's Voodoo Shop was unoccupied. Madame Delia was not around this time. The last time I was here, I hadn't taken notice of the unassuming two-story light pink building next door. Was it here then? The first doorway of the building sported a small beige sign that read Madame Delia's Spirits.

I hesitantly stepped inside the shop; the entrance flanked by tall, black wooden shutters weather-beaten by the salty Gulf Coast air. I hoped to find Madame Delia inside the store that bore her namesake.

The inside of the shop had the makings of an old general store protected from a phantom. Colorful beads and gris-gris cluttered the ceiling, forcing tall patrons to duck. Candles touting purity, protection, peace, and love filled small boxes like an old-fashioned mail slot. Voodoo dolls dressed in makeshift clothes intermixed with figurines of the Virgin Mary and crosses. Carved wooden masks hung from a metal rack gawked at me from the corner of the room. A few curious tourists perused the mystical trinkets.

Behind the glass display case full of cigars, the back of a stout woman faced me. She was in the process of adjusting the wall of wooden masks behind the counter. She had a similar figure and hair to Madame Delia, but I wasn't sure if it was her without seeing her face.

"Hello again, Will," the woman said to me, without turning around.

I gasped. "How did you know it was me?"

"There are many things that cannot be explained," Madame Delia replied, finally turning around to face me.

"But can you clarify somethin' for me?" I asked her.

164

When she inspected me with her esoteric eyes, a chill ran through me. Like the chill outside the LaLaurie Mansion.

"It depends," she said, resting on her cane. "Not everything can be explained."

Her vagueness infuriated me, but I couldn't let her see my ire.

"How do you know me?" I pressed, leaning on the glass countertop that separated us.

"I know a lot of shadows and spirits, but not all," Madame Delia quietly explained, raising nonagenarian arms to her sides. Her long flowing dress rippled in response. "Even those we cannot see."

"You're no help," I muttered under my breath.

"But I can be of help," she said, without shifting her face. "The same way you can assist me."

"How can *I* help you?" I arched an eyebrow at her.

"You have access to someone that I do not," Madame Delia explained with a somber face.

"You mean at Antoine's?" I couldn't imagine our clientele coming to this shop.

"No," she said. "In your world."

"What are you talking about?" I exclaimed, slamming my hand on the counter. The cigars on the shelf below rustled from the impact. "What world? I work at Antoine's."

165

"You will talk to someone for me and find out about her," Madame Delia explained. "Then I will help you."

"Who is this person you want me to talk to?" I said through gritted teeth. "And where do I find them?"

"You will know when you see her," she said.

"You want me to find someone I don't know, and I have to guess where she is?" I sneered.

"Yes." Madame Delia's ambiguous statements made my blood boil.

"If I find this person, what do I get in return?" I countered.

"I will give you the answers that you are seeking," she said.

Scoffing, I didn't have much of a choice. Madame Delia was the only one who could assist me to figure out how to tell Elle I knew her. And she knew it. Now she wanted me to help her find an unknown person in return, for reasons unbeknownst to me. Nothing made sense, especially the ramblings of the old woman in front of me. But my options were limited.

"Fine, I'll do it," I conceded.

"Very well," Madame Delia replied. "Remember... what you think is not what happened."

"What does *that* mean?" I wanted to know, biting back the urge to curse at her.

Instead of answering me, Madame Delia reached into a pocket of her flowing gown and pushed a crumpled black and white picture of a young girl in front of me. I presumed the girl to be around ten years old based on the plain, dark, school-age dress she wore. Her long blonde hair draped over her haunting eyes that didn't seem to focus on anything. What did she long for?

"Who is this?" I asked, picking up the old photo.

"You will find her for me," Madame Delia stated.

Then she slowly turned away from me, adjusting the wooden tiki masks on the wall behind her.

CHAPTER 22

My Darling,   19 January, 1864
    Today was almost an ill-fated day. I was crossing Esplanade Avenue talking to Monsieur DuBois and wasn't paying attention to where I was going. In a moment, he grasped me around the waist and pulled me to the ground as a streetcar narrowly missed me and trampled me to death. If it wasn't for Monsieur DuBois, I might have died and lost you forever. I am forever grateful to him for saving my

life. I cannot wait for you to meet him. He is a good man for taking me in as his apprentice. I hope you will agree when you meet him. I love you. You are lifeblood to me.

Yours forever,
Frédéric

Exasperated, I exited the spirit shop with more questions than answers. I headed east on St. Peter Street back toward Royal Street. St. Louis Cathedral towered over the block in front of me.

Who was the girl in the photo? How did Madame Delia know her? Was the girl her child? How would I find her? Why could Madame Delia not find her? If I found the girl, would Madame Delia follow through with her promise to help me? I still had no idea how to tell Elle I knew her, but Madame Delia was my only hope, and she was a far-reach at best.

Or was she?

Instead of making a right on Royal to go back to Antoine's, I made a left and walked a half-block toward the cathedral. Again, local artists hawked their wares along the black iron fence of the large church. I hooked a right onto Pirate Alley.

169

Had Elle not brought me here before, I would have missed Faulkner House Books. A pair of bashful blue, large, wooden, windowless doors blended into a grey brick wall. Ten feet up hanging from the underside of the second-story balcony, a small, mint green sign read `Faulkner House Books`. To the right of the blue doors, a bronze plaque read `Faulkner House, Here in 1925 William Faulkner Nobel Laureate wrote his first novel "Soldiers' Pay"`.

As I pulled the hefty door open, the door creaked as I stepped inside.

I ventured around the front room of the bookstore. Stacks of books balanced precariously to my right and left. Embedded shelves stretched floor to ceiling full of classic and local interest books.

"William Faulkner, is that you makin' noise again?" Mr. Howard emerged in the doorway from an adjoining room.

"No," William Faulkner replied. "It was my buddy, Will."

I gasped that he ruthlessly sold me out.

"That silly ghost," Mr. Howard grumbled when he didn't hear the response and turned back into the other room.

"I can't imagine you're here for books," William Faulkner said to me. He wore a heathered gray suit and a black tie. His full, dark eyebrows and bushy mustache

170

contrasted with the white hair on his head. The warm scent of a pipe lingered in the air.

"Um, no, I'm not," I replied, stunned that he remembered me. "How did you know?"

"We are aware of almost everything, Will," William Faulkner chuckled heartily. "Don't you know that?"

He was right; I couldn't help but chortle in return.

I pulled Madame Delia's photo from my pocket and presented it to him.

"Do you have any idea how I can figure out who this girl is?" I asked him.

"Possibly. Who gave you the photo?" William Faulkner asked.

"A fortune teller named Madame Delia," I replied.

"I've heard about her," he said. "She's the old woman who calls out random names on Jackson Square. She's a charlatan. Tourists are fond of her."

"I think she's the real deal," I said. "She knew who I was ... and I didn't tell her."

'Well... maybe she is legitimate." William Faulkner shrugged. "Let me see that photo." He took it and examined it closely. "My best guess is this girl was living in the 1890s. There is a horse-drawn market wagon in the street behind her. And she is here in the Quarter."

"Yeah, I figured that too," I said. "Any idea how I can find her?"

"Madame Delia wouldn't give you a hint?" he asked.

"No, nothing," I answered, annoyed. "She was vague. I need her help and she said she would assist me once I figure out this girl's story."

"Hmmm..." William Faulkner pondered. "Let's think about what was happening in New Orleans at that time."

"Antoine's was already 50 years old, I know that," I said.

"I was born in 1897 in Mississippi and didn't come to this city until 1925," he replied. "I wouldn't have been here at the same time."

"What about the Ursuline Convent?" I questioned. "That place has been around since the 1720s. They had kids there."

"Yes, but the nuns moved to the 9th Ward a hundred years later," he explained. "As you know, the original building is still on Chartres Street here in the Quarter, but the Archbishop moved into it in the late 19th century, so no children would have been around then."

Together, we examined the photo again.

"I have an idea, but it's a long shot," William Faulkner stated.

"Anythin' is worth a try," I said. "I'm desperate."

"If you head up the street here about a block away from the cathedral, there's an old hotel," he began.

"Yes, the Bourbon Orleans Hotel," I said. "I walked past it tryin' to find Madame Delia one day."

"The hotel used to be the Orleans Ballroom and Theater way back in the day and then it was turned into a convent and orphanage right around the timeframe you're talking about," William Faulkner explained. "If I were you, I'd go there and check things out."

"It's a good start," I said. "If nothin' else, I might get a lead to go somewhere else. Thank you." I turned away, heading for the door.

"My pleasure, Will," he said. "It's good to have a conversation with someone who can hear me. Come back any time."

"Thanks. I will." I turned back to face him. "Is it true that you grope the female staffers here?"

"A gentleman never tells." William Faulkner winked at me.

I left him in the bookstore and stepped into Pirate Alley, heading toward Royal Street.

CHAPTER 23

My Darling,   1 February, 1864
    Last night, I attended a dinner party with Monsieur DuBois at a home in the Garden District of New Orleans. I had never been in that section of the city because most of the French Creoles live in Vieux Carré. The Greek Revival house was beautiful with opulent white columns and a large front viewing porch. The owner is an investment broker in the cotton trade. I would

love to build a house like that for you. You deserve it, ma chérie.
Yours forever,
Frédéric

As much as I wanted to check out Bourbon Orleans Hotel, I decided to head back to Antoine's. The clock tower on the soaring cathedral spire behind me said 3:00. I had already skipped out on the lunch crowd and my coworkers wouldn't appreciate me missing the dinner rush.

Five minutes later, I entered Antoine's. The main and large annex dining rooms were ready and waiting for the public dinner crowd. All of the tables presented an angelic theme of white tablecloths, white china, and white napkins. Freshly shined silverware caught the reflection of the overhead chandeliers.

I pushed through the kitchen door and found Chef Miguel preparing Poulet sauce Rochambeau. Platters of chicken and ham laid on the metal counter in front of him. The rest of his staff chopped vegetables, made soups, and peeled crawfish. Large pots of water continuously boiled on the stove sending swirling clouds of steam into the air.

"What's goin' on, Will?" He stirred a pot of butter, flour, and cream for the sauce.

"Not much, Chef," I said, eyeing the small cauldron of Béarnaise sauce in front of him. "I'm lookin' for Terrance and Elle. Have you seen them?"

"I haven't seen Terrance in a while," Chef Miguel said. "But I sent Elle to the wine cellar a few minutes ago to get me a bottle of Grand Marnier."

"Thanks, Chef," I said. "I'll see ya later." I left him and headed down the hall to the wine cellar.

As I approached the wine cellar, someone was talking softly though I couldn't make out what was being said. I stopped and waited outside the door to listen as I recognized Terrance's voice. He said phrases like ".... Try it, you'll like it.... It'll make you feel so good... I promise you.... It won't hurt at all.... You won't regret it...."

Alarmed of what I might find, I feared the worst. Even though Terrance was my best friend, he couldn't have Elle. Not if I could help it. I stomped in and slammed the door against the frame, rattling the bottles of wine on the wall directly behind it. "What is goin' on..." I bellowed as I turned the corner to find Terrance and Elle, "... in here?" They huddled in the corner, sharing a small plate of cheesecake.

"What did you think we were doin'?" Terrance glared at me.

"I, um, I don't know..." I stuttered, embarrassed by my actions.

"Will, what's the matter with you?" Elle stared me down. "We aren't doin' anythin' except sharin' some dessert."

"Then why did I hear Terrance say, 'it'll make you feel so good'?" I defended myself.

"Because Elle told me she has been avoidin' sweets and I was tryin' to con her into eatin' this cheesecake," Terrance countered. "I was being funny."

"I'm so sorry, I thought..." I stammered, mortified that I let my jealousy get the best of me.

"What did you think, Will, that we were gettin' it on in here?" Terrance reprimanded me. "Get your mind out of the gutter. Besides, you know that we would both be fired."

"I'm sorry... I thought after what happened between you two last night that..." I stumbled, still embarrassed by my jumping to conclusions, "that, that somethin' was goin' on."

Elle huffed, pointing her finger at me. "Will, if I want to *engage* myself with someone, it's none of your damn business. Especially if it's Terrance." He gawked at her in flattery as if she read his mind. "But I can assure you, it won't be happenin' in the wine cellar!" She puffed out her chest and strutted off down the hall as fast as her short legs could take her.

"What's the matter, man?" Terrance lowered his voice. "You're actin' strange. Stranger than usual."

"I'm sorry. I had a weird mornin'," I told him, lowering my head in shame. "I'm so sorry. I visited that fortune teller this mornin' and now she is sendin' me all over the Quarter as payment for her to help me."

"I'll help you any way I can," Terrance told me. "You know that. I have your back." He paused a moment. "But if Elle flirts with me and says that she wants to *engage* with me, I'm not turnin' her down. I'm sorry, man, but I'm not."

"But..." I protested, raising a palm to him.

"Will, you know me," Terrance explained, staring me in the eye. "We've been friends for a long time. You know I would never purposely hurt her. I promise you that."

"Okay," I relinquished, realizing Terrance was right. He was a good man. The best. I was lucky to have him as my best friend. "But I still have to tell her how I know her. You know that it's been drivin' me crazy ever since I met her."

"I know."

Elle reappeared a few seconds later, interrupting Terrance and me. A grimace was still plastered on her face.

"Oops, I almost forgot this." She picked up a bottle of Grand Marnier from a nearby table and took off back down the hall.

178

CHAPTER 24

My Darling,   13 February, 1864
I wish I could pick you flowers. Something beautiful for the most beautiful woman I have ever met. I will plant your favorite white roses in our backyard, and they will be in full bloom by the time you arrive. I miss you so much.
Yours forever,
Frédéric

The next morning, Elle skipped into the main dining room where Terrance and I were setting up for lunch. A broad, toothy grin formed on her soft face.

"What are you so happy about?" I asked her. "After that earful you gave me yesterday…"

"I'm over that," Elle replied, brushing her hand at me. "You'll never guess who called me this mornin'."

"The manager at The Spotted Cat?" Terrance offered. "He wants you to sing there every month?"

"Oh god no," Elle answered. "I was terrified enough as it was singin' in front of everyone one time. No way could I do it on a regular basis. You'd have to get a lot of whisky in me for that to happen."

"Challenge accepted," Terrance replied.

Elle stared him down, warning him to drop it.

"Then who was it?" I asked, going back to the topic.

"The owner at New Orleans Watchmakers," Elle told us. "He called and said he has a lead on the pocket watch from the antique picture."

"And you didn't think he was pullin' through for you," I replied with a smirk. Part of me wanted to support her treasure hunt and the other part of me wanted to prevent her from finding out the truth. I would eventually tell her everything, but not yet.

"He wants me to come back down to his shop so that he can show me in person what he found," Elle said, then turned to me. "Will, you want to come with me again?"

"Yeah, I'd love to," I told her. I originally had plans to check out Bourbon Orleans Hotel today, but that could wait. I wanted to spend time with Elle.

"Good," she said. "I already asked about takin' a couple of hours off today in between lunch and dinner, so we can go as soon as lunch is over. But I wasn't sure if you could go, so I didn't ask for you."

"Don't worry, I'll be fine," I replied. "They usually let me take a break whenever I want."

"What're they gonna do? Fire you?" Terrance jested.

Elle scrunched up her nose at us in a confused expression because she didn't get the joke.

* * *

A few hours later, after the last lunch patron spooned up their last bite of chocolate mousse, Elle and I headed to the watch shop. With no time to change her clothes, she still wore the standard-issue black tuxedo and black bow tie. Her dark hair was pulled up tightly into several layers of thick braids twisted into a crown around her head.

After making a right out of Antoine's and taking the first left onto Bourbon Street, Elle blew out a long breath and tugged at her starched collar. "This heat is brutal today," she groaned, wiping a bead of sweat from her forehead. "Why do I never hear you complain about it?"

"I don't know," I said. "I've lived here a long time and I guess I've gotten used to it."

"One of these days you'll have to tell me your secret." Elle removed her jacket, folded it inward to prevent wrinkles, and draped it over her arm.

The crowd on Bourbon Street was pretty calm for the afternoon. A few tourists took pictures of the horizon of the street stretching far ahead of them. Construction workers filled a large, red Dumpster in front of Galatoire's Restaurant. The bars promoting Big Easy daiquiris and beers enjoyed their afternoon naps before the mass of partiers came after dark.

Elle and I traveled toward the beginning of Bourbon Street, crossed Canal Street, and headed for New Orleans Watchmakers on the next block.

Five minutes later, Elle and I pushed through the shop door.

"Hello again," Elle said to the owner who was busy performing surgery on a watch that was near death's door.

"Thank you for coming back," he said, viewing her through magnifying spectacles. "Give me one more minute to finish up." He made another adjustment on the old timepiece, wiped his hands on a nearby cloth, and removed the Jules Verne-era glasses from his face.

He spoke to Elle again, "I hope I have some good news for you. I made a few phone calls asking around if anyone could give me a lead. This search was like finding a needle in a haystack. I'm not sure if it's exactly what you're asking for, but I hope it will help you."

"I know I didn't give you much to go on." Elle lowered her head. "All I gave you was the 1860s to work with. But I truly appreciate you tryin'."

"I hope it was enough," the shop owner replied. "During that time, the city of New Orleans was a bustling port. Ships came in from Europe all the time sending goods up the Mississippi River, all the way to Chicago."

Elle smiled impatiently at the man, hoping he would tell his story a little faster.

He continued, "The men in charge of the products going in and out of the port were called commission merchants. Much like the modern-day car salesman, they got a cut of the profit of the goods going in and out of the port. Usually one or two percent."

"What does a commission merchant have to do with the pocket watch in my photo?" Elle begged the question.

"It turns out that one of the more successful commission merchants in the 1860s was a gentleman by the name of Pierre DuBois," the shop owner replied.

A small gasp escaped my lips. I stood behind Elle; thankful she couldn't see the distress on my face.

"I've never heard of him," Elle replied, more intrigued by the story than my random pant. "Who was he?"

"He owned several buildings in the Quarter back then, one of which was a men's boutique along St. Louis Street," the store owner told her. "It was a pretty well-known shop then. He sold clothing, shoes, hats, and, of course, watches."

"That's where Antoine's is," Elle added.

"Yes, exactly," the shop owner said. "The boutique was on the 800 block, near where the Hermann-Grima House still is today."

Elle chuckled, "And to think we could have stayed on St. Louis Street all this time, instead of runnin' all over the Quarter."

"Yeah, maybe," the man told her. "But as I said, I'm not sure if it's exactly what you're looking for."

"It's better than nothin'," Elle replied. "I honestly didn't expect you to find anythin'. But this could work out. Do you think this Pierre DuBois might have sold the man in my picture the pocket watch?"

"It's possible," the shop owner said. "If I were you, I'd stop in the Hermann-Grima House museum. They might have some info on the old boutique since it was on the same block. Maybe they can direct you to an original list of the shop's clientele? A lot of shops kept records of their best customers back then. You never know what they might have. I wish I had more for you."

"Thank you," Elle gushed. "You've done more than enough for me. I appreciate it." She reached across the display case and shook the shop owner's hand.

"Good luck," he told her. "I hope you find your answers."

"Thank you," Elle replied.

I followed her out the door and back to work.

CHAPTER 25

My Darling,   25 February, 1864

This morning, while I was working at the port, one of the ship captains gave me an oak sapling from his cargo ship. He told me to plant it in our backyard so that you and I can grow old together underneath its shade. Right now, it barely reaches the top of the roof. I cannot wait to lie beneath it with you watching our future children play.

Yours forever,
Frédéric

The next evening, on hiatus from the dinner crowd at Antoine's, I headed down Bourbon Street toward Bourbon Orleans Hotel. The night sea of people along the narrow street brought on an acute case of claustrophobia. Many years ago, the city police had the good foresight to block off Bourbon Street from vehicles to prevent even more congestion and noise.

I dodged a group of 20-something guys imbibing on a mixture of vodka, gin, and rum from the well-known plastic, green hand grenades from one of the nightclubs on Bourbon Street that made the drink. Buildings that had snoozed during the day came alive with flamingo-colored neon signs. Rock music reverberated out of bars as bands began their sets. As groups of drunk bachelorette parties stumbled down the street, I silently said a prayer to the Creole gods that I could work most nights and didn't have to deal with this chaos.

As I crossed Toulouse and then St. Peter Street, the thoroughfare crowd lessened to white noise and I could breathe again. Even though the sun had been down for a couple of hours, the late summer heat hadn't dissipated.

At the next corner, the intersection of Bourbon and Orleans Streets, six stories of white lights illuminated Bourbon Orleans Hotel. Plantation-style shutters and private wrought-iron second-floor galleries accented the grand, green and white building. An old, bronze sign to the left of the main entrance read: Former Site of Holy Family Sisters' Convent. The Old Orleans Ballroom, built in 1817, served a number of purposes over the decades. Its most unique function was as a convent, orphanage, and school of the Sisters of the Holy Family.

Hoping to find some kind of information on the girl in Madame Delia's photo, I opened the lobby door and slipped inside. Several massive, multi-tiered, gold and crystal chandeliers hung from the ceiling above me. A few guests chatted quietly on the orange and gold sofas. Forest green, marble pillars supporting the second floor stretched down the long lobby.

From the stories I heard around the Quarter, Bourbon Orleans Hotel was haunted by a confederate soldier on the sixth floor, a lonely dancer in the main ballroom, and by several children and nuns who wandered the floors. I wasn't sure what I'd find, but I pressed on so that Madame Delia could eventually help me.

Going unnoticed, I headed down the hall toward the banquet rooms that housed the former medical ward and school rooms. The hallway was empty except for a young girl in a pink smock rolling a red ball down the carpet. Her hair was pulled back in two braids attached by a ribbon at the ends. Matching bloomers peeked out from under the hem of her dress.

"Hi!" she said to me, glancing over her shoulder while chasing the rubber ball. "Wanna play wiff me?"

"Umm..." I pointed to myself and peered to both sides of me to see if anyone was behind me. "Are you talkin' to me?"

"Yes, silly," she said with bright green eyes. "I'm Lizabiff," she lisped. "What's your name?"

"You can call me Will," I told her. I gazed down the empty hall. "Elizabeth, where are your parents?" I asked her, hoping she wasn't out here playing alone.

"Don't know, Mr. Will." She shrugged and half-giggled. "I was dropped here when I was two. The nice sisters have been taking care of me ever since. I'm six now." She proudly puffed out her chest and pushed her fists into her tiny waist.

Ah, the sisters. Now it all made sense. I pulled Madame Delia's photo out of my pocket and squatted down on the carpet in front of the precocious little girl. "Can you help me?" I asked her.

"Sure!" Elizabeth smiled at me with a mouthful of missing teeth.

"Do you know this girl?" I asked, putting the picture in front of her.

"Hmmm...." She scrunched her eyebrows and nose as if she was thinking hard. "Maybe..."

"Try and remember," I encouraged her.

She studied the photo for a few silent seconds. "I don't know," she finally said. "Maybe Sister Fwances would know?"

"Who is Sister Frances?" I asked her, standing up straight.

"She's my teacher!"

Before I could protest, Elizabeth grabbed my hand and dragged me down the hall, abandoning her ball.

A few moments later, we approached an emerald green double door laden with gold trim. Elizabeth reached up and opened the door with her free hand and led me over the threshold with her other. I clutched Madame Delia's photo in my free hand.

A slight gasp escaped my mouth as soon as we stepped inside the large room.

In front of me, ghostly nuns in black habits scurried around a line of beds full of sick children swaddled under blankets. Spectral nurses in white dresses and face masks carried sick babies in their arms soothing them. A priest in long robes gave last rights to a dying child in the makeshift hospital. A stench similar to rotting meat in a butcher shop made me gag.

"There's Sister Fwances," Elizabeth said, tugging on my hand. With her other hand, she pointed to a nun in the far corner of the room taking the temperature of a young frail boy who lay ashen on a bed in front of her. I stood silently and watched; my mouth agape. Where was

I? And how could Elizabeth have such a happy demeanor in a woeful place like this? Dread tried to consume me, but I fought it off, remembering thankfully I didn't belong there. I was able to leave but none of them could.

Elizabeth guided me around a row of beds toward the nun. I raised my hand to my mouth at the misery around me. We approached the sister from behind and Elizabeth yanked on her habit to get the nun's attention.

The holy woman turned around and spoke sternly when she recognized who tugged on her clothes. "Elizabeth, what have I told you about pulling on my robes?"

"Sorry, Sister Fwances." Elizabeth shamefully lowered her eyes. "I fugot."

The woman took notice of me and said, "Can I help you?" Her weary yellow eyes were battered from the exhaustion of tending to the sick children and teaching the healthy ones.

"This is Mr. Will," Elizabeth spoke for me, raising her chin.

"Yes," I said. "Please call me Will." I surveyed the ailing children around the room. "I'm sorry to bother you, but I was wonderin' if you could help me locate a child."

"I will do what I can," Sister Frances replied.

I presented Madame Delia's crumpled black and white photo to the nun. "Do you know this girl?"

191

Sister Frances sighed heavily. "Yes, I'm afraid I do," she said, then eyed me suspiciously. "Why do you want to know?"

My heart raced in a panic. I couldn't lie to a woman of the cloth. Nor could I tell her the whole truth because I didn't know all of the answers myself.

"I'm askin' for a friend who couldn't come here and ask herself," I finally blurted. "Do you know where I can find the girl?"

The old woman studied me with narrowed eyes, then spoke. Hopefully, she trusted me with information that she knew.

"Her name was Maria Dinu."

"Was?" I feared the worst.

"Yes, the Good Lord called her home. Maria died here a few months ago of yellow fever. She was fifteen," the nun explained. "She was a pleasant girl, always happy. Her family brought her, actually no, it wasn't her family because her real family was still in Romania. She was one of the few from that country. I later learned the people who brought her here were her employers, but you could tell she adored them as if she was related to them. Her parents in Romania sent her to New Orleans to be an au pair for the other family. That family's name was Baillairgé. She had worked for them for a few years."

Sister Frances wiped a small tear from her eye and kissed the rosary hanging from her neck.

I wasn't sure how Maria's story related to Madame Delia, but I openly listened to Sister Frances. Elizabeth quietly stood by my side.

Sister Frances continued, "The Baillairgés brought Maria here when she fell sick. Madame Baillairgé came every day to sit with Maria. A week after she passed, they buried her in St. Louis Cemetery No. 1."

"Thank you, Sister." I grasped her hand in both of mine and shook it. "You've been a great help."

"God bless you," she replied. "I have something else that might help you."

"What is it, Sister?" I asked.

"A few days after Maria died," she told me, "Monsieur and Madame Baillairgé brought their daughter Adélaïde here, too. She was also sick with the fever. She died a couple of days later and they buried Adélaïde a week after Maria. It was such a shame they lost two young girls at once. They eventually left the city for the countryside with their remaining children to avoid the mosquitoes."

"How awful. I couldn't even imagine what they went through," I said. "Thank you so much, Sister Frances. I appreciate everythin' you've told me."

"You're welcome," the nun replied. "May the Lord bless you on your search."

I turned and headed toward the hospital room door; Elizabeth was on my heels. As I reached for the door handle, she tugged on my pant leg.

"Oh, sorry." She scrunched her hands into tiny fists, realizing her mistake. "I fugot again."

"Yes, Elizabeth?"

"Will you stay and play with me?" she asked, with pleading eyes.

"I'm afraid I have to go back to work," I told her. "Next time I see you, I'll play with you. I promise."

"Okay," Elizabeth said. "Goodbye, Mr. Will."

"Goodbye, Elizabeth."

I opened the double door, stepped over the threshold, and re-entered the hallway of Bourbon Orleans Hotel.

CHAPTER 26

My Darling,   10 March, 1864
    Last night, I attended a brass band performance at a theatre. Lovely sounds from trumpets, trombones, and clarinets reminded me of the musicians we listened to when we traveled to Paris. The Daily Picayune newspaper wrote an article several years back that complained about the emergence of brass bands on every corner of Vieux Carré. I think the music in this city

is wonderful and I cannot wait for you to hear it.

Yours forever,
Frédéric

The next morning before work, I headed to St. Louis Cemetery No. 1, five blocks northwest of Antoine's, at the corner of St. Louis and Basin Streets. The cemetery was the oldest extant burial ground in the city dating back to the late 1700s. Unique to the below-sea-level city of New Orleans, the above-ground tombs were a necessity with the constant threat of flooding.

Even as the morning sun reflected off the marble tombs creating an angelic glow, I shuddered at the thought of wandering a maze of thousands of dead bodies around me. I preferred the company of the living that was for sure.

The cemetery was also considered to be the most haunted one in the United States. A few years back, the Archdiocese was forced to halt visiting hours by the general public. Nosy tourists and taphophiles had vandalized the supernatural crypts hoping to see the ghosts of voodoo queen Marie Laveau, nomad sailor Henry Vignes, sugarcane tycoon Etienne de Bore, first governor of Louisiana William C.C. Claiborne, and chess champion Paul Morphy.

When the undeterred scaled the ominous cemetery walls after dark, they often came face to face with local police who arrested them on the spot. Now, only licensed tour groups approved by the Archdiocese and descendants of the dead could enter the cemetery.

On a mission, I slipped inside the gate, joining the tail end of a group, and plodded along the broken shell and cobblestone path between the crumbling and chipped above-ground tombs. The cemetery danced melodically between beauty and ruin. With a disorganized network of multi-sized crypts in front of me, I guessed that only the resident ghosts and groundskeepers could easily navigate what Mark Twain once called "The City of the Dead".

With the cemetery gate to my back, I blew out a frustrating sigh. How would I ever find the tomb of young Maria Dinu? A labyrinth of tombs spread out before me, in different sizes and shapes. Maria didn't die with her Romanian family so I assumed she would have been buried in a mass tomb. Hopefully, her final resting place was marked with her name. With many of the older crypts missing nameplates, I couldn't be sure.

I headed left, disembarking from the tour group going right. Beside me, a three-level wall made up the exterior border of the cemetery. Each level had two-foot by two-foot indented sections for each person buried within the wall. Some of the sections were engraved with a family name, most were not. Several of the small ledges along the wall supported small vases of flowers to honor the dead inside.

What could Madame Delia do to me if I didn't find out where Maria Dinu was buried? I believed she was a legitimate priestess and could converse with the dead. I was on her good side for now and she never threatened me, but I feared what she could conjure up if I failed her. Would she send a voodoo demon after me? Even if I didn't go back to her shop, she still knew how to find me. I shuddered at the thought.

At the end of the front wall, I turned right, more disintegrating crypts in front of me. Nameplates of Ortiz and Leccacie caught my eye, but not Dinu.

I ventured into the maze of the tombs, heading toward the multi-storied crypts. The first one I approached was a four-level round mausoleum with a statue of the Virgin Mary, sans a right hand, seated at the front. Beneath her, an engraved marble plate read Italia. A small bronze plaque to the left indicated this massive tomb was for the Italian Benevolent Society of New Orleans. The society provided cheap burials for Italian immigrants in New Orleans in the early 20th century. Maybe a smaller monument existed for the former, lesser-known Romanian residents of the city?

Several small tour groups wandered in front of me. Most of the onlookers took pictures of the eerie vaults but were unaware of the mystical spirits who watched them.

The tour groups gawked at the clashing, empty, glistening, white pyramid tomb of actor Nicolas Cage that took up four normal size grave plots. He bought the parcel in 2010 with the intent to be buried here, even though he no longer lived in the city. The plaque on the front of the controversial tomb read Omnia Ab Uno which translated to Everything from One.

I continued my search.

Several cemetery alleys behind the pyramid tomb, a plain, squared, six-level tomb took precedence over surrounding meager crypts. I found the marble plate on the side that read Eastern European. Could Maria Dinu be buried here? This otherwise unmarked mausoleum was my best hope. Canvassing the rest of the cemetery seemed daunting and futile to me. Madame Delia would have to accept what I found. If she wasn't pleased, I accepted my fate.

I made my way back through the maze of crypts, to the cemetery gate.

"Are you lost, dear?" a voice called to me from behind.

Startled, I turned around to see an older woman in a black, plain mourning dress. A dark veil partially covered her face. She held a bunch of fresh flowers in her black-gloved hands. A black onyx necklace hung around her neck. I stared at her, unblinking. None of the nearby tour groups took notice of the elderly woman in front of me.

"These are for my husband," she told me, glancing toward her armful of red roses. "He died of the fever. I know this place can be hard to navigate sometimes if you don't know where you are going." She gestured to the tombs around us. "Did you find what you were searching for?"

"Um, yes, I think so," I stuttered, still startled that she spoke to me. "But maybe you can help me?"

"I will try," she told me.

I pulled Madame Delia's photo out of my pocket and presented it to the helpful woman. "I'm tryin' to find this girl. Her name is Maria Dinu and she is of Romanian descent. I was told she was buried here. I found the eastern European mausoleum, but the crypt isn't marked well so I'm not sure if she is there."

The kind widow examined the weathered black and white photo in my fingers. "Yes, I've seen her here. She tends to a young girl named Adélaïde. Their crypt is worn because it's so old, but the nameplate used to say, 'Our beloved daughters Maria and Adélaïde Baillairgé.'"

That was the same surname that Sister Frances told me. I forgot that the girls had been buried at the same time. I had ventured into the wrong section of the cemetery. I still wasn't sure how all the names converged together, but Madame Delia would have to sort it all out.

200

The old woman gestured behind her. "They are in the next section. I can show you if you want."

"Yes, that would be helpful," I replied. I followed the mourning woman through an aisle between two marble crypts.

The widow pointed down the cobblestone path and I followed her gaze. "Their tomb is the fifth one on the left."

"Thank you very much," I told the woman as I headed toward Maria's crypt. "You've been a big help."

"Good, I'm happy to assist," she said. "Maybe I'll see you around here again." With that, she headed toward the cemetery border wall and disappeared into it.

CHAPTER 27

My Darling,   21 March, 1864
    Today I tried a Cajun meal. I
had been eating Creole food since I
arrived but have now been introduced
to Cajun and it is just as delicious.
What is the difference, you may ask?
Creole food is a blend of the various
cultures of New Orleans including
French, Italian, Spanish, African,
German,   Caribbean,   Native
American, and Portuguese. Cajun
food   is   the   provincial   country
cousin. Creoles have access to more

exotic ingredients like butter, remoulade sauce, and tomatoes, while Cajun does not. Cajun cooking uses The Holy Trinity of onions, bell peppers, and celery to provide a flavour base for many dishes. I cannot wait to share a meal with you in this wonderful city. We have many years ahead of us to eat together.

Yours forever,
Frédéric

When I entered Antoine's fifteen minutes later, the restaurant was abuzz with staff getting ready for the lunch crowd. I found Georgia and Charles setting up the table in the Rex private dining room. She pulled wine glasses out of a crate and handed them to him to arrange on the table. Other wait staff swept the floor, made sure silverware lay perfect on the table, and refolded wilting napkins.

"What's goin' on?" I asked them.

"Did you forget?" Charles admonished me, crystal glasses in his hands. "Where have you been?"

"The mayor and her staff are coming for lunch today," Georgia spoke sternly. Twenty-five place settings dotted the oval table under the crystal chandelier in the gold and emerald room. "Get your butt moving and help us. Everything has to be more than perfect."

"Oh.... I... Oh..." I stammered, stupefied by my coworkers bustling around like worker bees jockeying to get to the hive queen. "I completely forgot. I'm so sorry."

I rushed over to them, grabbed wine bottles out of the boxes, and straightened each one on the table so the label faced forward like a line of glass soldiers in formation. Charles had made a special pitcher of Sazerac for the occasion and placed it next to the wine bottles.

Terrance and Elle pushed through the dining room doors carrying silver platters full of Oysters Rockefeller and potato soufflés. As they set the trays on a table next to mine, they talked in hushed tones, intimately, as if they didn't notice me. Terrance set his tray down first and then grabbed the tray out of Elle's arms. As his hand grazed hers, she smiled at him.

As I stopped mid-motion putting a wine bottle on the table, a pang of jealousy jolted inside me. Did I miss something while I was out on my search? Elle and Terrance lingered closer than they ever had as if they shared a secret they weren't telling anyone. Did Elle renege on her no dating coworkers rule? A fire of jealousy burned inside me.

"Hey, Will," Terrance finally acknowledged me. He eyed me up and down. "Where've ya been?"

"I had to do somethin'," I said, keeping my answer ambiguous so that Elle didn't ask questions that I wasn't ready to answer.

"Today of all days?" Elle scolded me. "You knew the mayor was comin' today. Chef Miguel has been remindin' us for the past week. He even put a sign up in the kitchen."

"I'm sorry," I sputtered. "I forgot."

Elle blew out an annoyed sigh. "Will, I swear some days you are somewhere else."

"I'm doin' it all for the right reasons. Believe me," I told her.

Elle dismissed me with a quick wave of her hand and headed back out the door to get another tray of appetizers. Terrance followed her like a puppy dog, or maybe it was my imagination.

"Why are you starin' at them like that?" Charles asked me, as he wiped a spotted knife. He noticed my long gaze when Elle and Terrance left the room. "They seem cute together."

"It's complicated," I groaned. "Very complicated."

"Well," Charles replied, "when you're ready to talk, I'll listen. That's part of my job requirement."

I chuckled at Charles's occupational humor.

A half-hour later, Mayor Correlle and her entourage nibbled on oysters and potatoes around the table. A graduate of Harvard's Kennedy School of Government, Lydia Correlle was the first woman to hold the esteemed post. Mayor Correlle was given a lifetime achievement award by the presidents of Tulane, Loyola, and Xavier Universities, and the University of New Orleans for her service to the community. Chef Miguel presented his best dishes to her as his gratitude from the resilient city.

While the mayor and her staff dined and discussed their plans for the city over main courses of Shrimp Rémoulade and Filet de Gulf Poisson Amandine, Elle, Terrance and I waited in the kitchen.

"Did you see that we're all off on Sunday?" Elle spoke. "What are y'all doin' then? Do you have any plans?"

"I don't know yet," I told her. My schedule for my next free day was dependent on what Madame Delia told me the next time I saw her.

"Me either," Terrance said. "Why?"

"Well..." Elle explained. "If you're interested, my daddy has invited both of y'all to Sunday dinner at my parents' house in Bywater. He liked y'all. All of my siblings will be there."

"I'd love to meet the rest of your family," Terrance immediately spoke. His admiring gaze held her for an extra second and he discreetly grazed her arm with a finger.

Elle blushed sheepishly in response.

"Me too," I quickly replied, noticing the unspoken tête-à-tête between them. I wanted to learn more about Elle and her clan. Maybe being around them could help me figure out how to explain everything to her? But Terrance would be there too. Jealousy boiled deep inside me again.

"We already met Nina and Nat," Terrance said. "What are your other siblings' names?"

"Louie, Sarah, and Billie," Elle answered.

"Wait... Louie, Sarah, Billie... and Elle, Nina, and Nat?" I questioned, as my mind conjured up why I recognized all those names.

"Yes," Elle said, reading my mind. "We were all named after famous musicians."

"You're serious?" Terrance stifled a laugh, running his finger lightly along her arm again.

"Yes," Elle replied, with a smile. "We're named after Louis Armstrong, Sarah Vaughan, Billie Holiday, Ella Fitzgerald, Nina Simone, and Nat King Cole. My parents wanted the music tradition to carry on in their kids' lives even if we all didn't end up singin' and playin' like they did."

"But Nat and Nina did," I stated.

"Yes, and they were the only ones," Elle replied. "Sarah is an EMT, Billie works for the Red Cross, Louie is a senior at Tulane..."

"And you're here," Terrance finished Elle's sentence, smiling at her.

"Yes," Elle said, blushing again. "With our odd schedules, we all try to get together for Sunday dinner once a month. My parents live on Desire Street in Bywater. It's a twenty-minute ride by streetcar from here."

Elle cringed at her faux pas. "Sorry, Will. I forgot you don't do streetcars."

"It's okay," I told her.

"We can get a cab," Terrance piped up.

I was grateful that Terrance covered for me once again despite our obvious competition for Elle's affections.

"What should I bring?" Terrance asked.

"Nothin'," Elle said. "My mama makes more than enough. But you have to try her collard greens. They're the best I've ever had. Don't tell Chef Miguel."

I gulped down a pocket of air. I didn't eat collard greens, but I didn't want to insult Elle's mother either. What was I going to do?

CHAPTER 28

My Darling,   1 April, 1864
    Tonight, I stopped in Alexis
Coffee House at the intersection of
des Rues Bourbon and Bienville to
get some libations after working at
the port. As I struck up a
conversation with the owner, he told
me the interesting history of the
building. A Spanish couple erected
the building in 1807 and established
their business of importers of
foodstuffs and wine from Spain.
Later, the building was a shoe shop, a

grocery store, and now the current coffeehouse where they serve green Absinthe. Fifty years ago, American General and later President Andrew Jackson commissioned pirate Jean Lafitte and his band of buccaneers in that building to win the Battle of New Orleans to help win the War of 1812. This city is already full of rich history. I cannot wait to share it with you. I miss you so much. You are always in my heart.

     Yours forever,
     Frédéric

The next morning, Elle found me in Hermes Bar talking to Charles. She pursed her lips, sidled up to the bar, and draped her arms on the countertop in front of us.

"You look troubled," Charles said to her from behind the bar.

"How did you know?" Elle replied.

"It's part of my job," Charles said. "I have a sixth sense about these things."

I chuckled at his joke.

"What's on your mind?" Charles asked Elle, as he wiped the counter in front of her with a white cloth.

"Well..." she began, "it's more about somethin' that happened with Will."

"With me?" I cringed. I hadn't told her about my scavenger hunt for Madame Delia so I couldn't imagine what Elle was talking about.

"Yes," she said to me. "I was thinkin' more about that vintage portrait of the man with the pocket watch. The owner at the watchmakers told me to head to the Hermann-Grima House museum down the block."

"They had a fundraiser there last month," Charles interjected.

"Yes, that place," Elle replied. "Will, you know that picture has been botherin' me ever since I saw it. I want to go to the Hermann-Grima House museum and see what they can tell me. Do you want to come with me again?"

"Yes, of course," I said. Any alone time with Elle was worth the wild goose chase.

"We can go right after the lunch crowd is done," she said, cocking her head to the side. "Since it's up on the next block, we'll be back in plenty of time to set up for dinner."

* * *

211

Three hours later, I met Elle on the sidewalk in front of Antoine's and we headed right, toward the Hermann-Grima House.

In two minutes, we stood in front of the red-brick Federal-style former mansion, an uncommonly used architecture in early 19th century New Orleans. The historic house, now turned museum, had the only extant horse stable and 1830s open-hearth kitchen in the French Quarter. The wealthy Samuel Hermann built the structure in 1831 and then sold the home in 1844 to the cultured Judge Felix Grima and his family. The last members of the Grima family lived in the residence until 1921 when they sold it to The Christian Woman's Exchange who used the property as a boarding house for single women. The building was restored and opened as a museum in 1975.

I followed Elle as she climbed the three cement steps to the oak double doors of the main entrance. The curves of her backside engrossed me. She was lovely.

A bronze plaque to the left of the entrance promoted the building's declaration of a National Historic Landmark. Elle pushed the doors open and we crossed the threshold to a building that modern New Orleans barely noticed anymore.

The extravagant lifestyle of an affluent Creole family displayed before us. Airy lace curtains hung from the floor-to-ceiling windows. Dense crystal chandeliers suspended from the ceiling above us. Gilded portraits of the original family members guarded plush red pillar and scroll sofas. A pair of antique bronze inkwells perched on the corners of a 19th century mahogany desk. Large vases of flowers and cherub marble statues sat atop credenzas along the perimeter of the parlor. Bookcases filled with vintage editions completed the collection. As Elle and I slowly browsed around the room, our feet shuffled along summer seagrass mats.

A blonde, older woman in a yellow sundress approached us from an adjoining room. "Hello, can I help you?" she asked Elle.

"Yes, ma'am," Elle said. "I hope so. Do you know anythin' about the old shops that used to be along this block in the 1860s?"

"We might," the woman told her. "We primarily have the history of this house and its former owners. We have some information on the nearby properties. What are you looking for, specifically?"

The thought suddenly hit me. Elle could go to the Beauregard-Keyes House for answers. The building was now a museum and tour spot. But I wouldn't suggest going there until I had answers myself.

Elle took a quick breath. "The short answer is I'd like information about a man from that time by the name of Pierre DuBois. He apparently owned a men's clothin' boutique along this block durin' the 1860s. Do you know anythin' about him?"

"That name doesn't sound familiar to me," the woman said. "However, the museum shop is right outside on the other side of the courtyard. Go inside and talk to Kailey. She is our curator and resident history expert."

"Thank you," Elle replied, shaking the woman's hand. Elle turned on her heels and I followed her out the front door.

Thirty seconds later, we stepped inside the museum shop and approached the front desk.

"Hello," a middle-aged woman with a name tag `Kailey` on her chest addressed Elle with a broad smile. "Would you like to purchase a tour ticket?"

"No, ma'am," Elle said, sheepishly. "I'm on a break from work and I'll have to come back another time for a tour. But I was wonderin' if you could help me?"

"I will try," Kailey replied.

"Do you know anythin' about a man named Pierre DuBois?" Elle asked her. "He owned a shop on this block in the 1860s."

Kailey gave Elle a thoughtful look. "The name doesn't sound familiar, but that doesn't mean we can't find out. Can you tell me more?"

"He was a commission merchant durin' that time who owned a men's clothin' shop somewhere along this block, but I don't know which buildin'." Elle motioned toward the street through the museum shop windows.

214

"Most of the buildings on this street have changed hands over the years so I have no idea which one was his."

"Okay," Kailey said. "That's a good start. Tell me more."

Elle heaved a hopeful sigh. "I recently purchased a vintage portrait from an antique shop across from Jackson Square. I didn't bring it with me, but the man in the photo seems so familiar to me. I can't get over it. Anyway, he is standin' in front of the Beauregard-Keyes House. I've been to The Historic Collection, Keil's Antiques, and the owner of New Orleans Watchmakers suggested I talk to y'all. His thought was that Pierre DuBois was associated with the man in the picture. I still have yet to go to the Beauregard-Keyes House to ask them though. I've been all over the Quarter tryin' to figure out who this guy is. I feel like I've met him before. It's not possible, right?" Elle silently begged for the woman's help with her wide aquamarine eyes.

Kailey reached beneath the desk and put a thick album on the counter in front of Elle. "Maybe this will help?"

She flipped open a few pages to old photos and articles that reflected the beginnings of the city. I recognized Old Chartres Street, the French Market, Jackson Square, and the cathedral. Kailey found the page highlighting the Hermann-Grima House.

Kailey pointed to a worn newspaper article dated 1859 and leaned in to examine it further. "It says here the Grima family's neighbors consisted of a milliner, an apothecary, and a coffeehouse. No word of a men's clothier. But that doesn't mean it didn't exist. It means that Mr. Grima didn't talk about it in this news article." Kailey gazed up at Elle. "The family left New Orleans during The War of Northern Aggression and fled to Augusta, Georgia. Union troops commandeered the home for the next few years, then the Grimas came back."

Kailey abruptly stopped talking, raised her chin, and sniffed the air. "Do you smell the roses?" she asked Elle.

"Yes, a little," Elle replied and glanced around the room but didn't see a vase. "But you don't have any here. Where's the smell comin' from?"

Kailey grinned. "Those are Mrs. Grima's. She loved roses. The aroma is not too heavy today, but guests here have told me that the scent was so strong they thought we had roses in the centerpieces when we didn't."

Elle gave me a side glance. She clearly had not yet been converted to a believer.

Kailey continued, "Several of our former residents still linger here. They don't bother us because they are well-mannered like they were when they were alive and continue to share their welcoming hospitality."

Elle's eyes glazed over at the mystical tale.

216

"Anyway," Kailey said, noticing Elle's disinterest. "I'm sorry I don't have any good information for you on Pierre DuBois or his clothing shop."

"It's okay," Elle replied, with a half-smile. "I appreciate you tryin'. You've done more than enough. Thank you."

"You're welcome," Kailey said.

I followed Elle out of the museum shop and we stopped on the sidewalk in front of the aging red brick building.

She heaved a heavy sigh and lowered her shoulders in disappointment. "I honestly thought they would have had somethin' for me."

"I know you did," I told her. I wanted to take her in my arms and squeeze out her frustration.

"There's somethin' about that guy in the photo," Elle fretted, her wide eyes glossing over with tears. "I know I've seen him somewhere else. I know it."

"You'll figure it out soon," I assured her.

"I hope so," Elle said. "I've come to a dead end. I don't know what else to do or where to go. But still feel like we're connected somehow."

Seeing Elle crushed hurt my heart. I knew who the man in the picture was, but I wasn't ready to tell her. I needed to talk to Madame Delia first. But before that, I couldn't wait to meet the rest of Elle's family at dinner on Sunday.

CHAPTER 29

My Darling,   *10 April, 1864*

Tonight, I went to the French Opera House to see a performance by Edmund Dédé. It is a lovely building at the corner of des Rues Bourbon and Toulouse. It was designed by the same architect who built the Pontalba Buildings for Baroness Micaela Almonester Pontalba along Jackson Square fifteen years ago. The grand auditorium was decorated in red and white and it seated two thousand people in four tiers. I wish you could have been there with me. Everyone would have been staring at you because you are so beautiful. I miss you so much, ma chérie.

Yours forever,
Frédéric

On Sunday, a cab dropped Terrance and me along Desire Street in Bywater. Contrary to popular Yankee misconception, the street was not named after the streetcar line in Tennessee Williams's famous play. The road was given its moniker in dedication to Désirée Gautier Montrieul, the daughter of Robert Gautier de Montrieul who owned the plantation on the land where the street now runs. The streetcar line was named for the narrow avenue. Many of the homes at this end of Desire Street had been destroyed by Hurricane Katrina, but several, including Elle's parents', were restored to their former glory.

"How do I look?" Terrance asked me as we stopped on the sidewalk as the cab drove away. Terrance wore navy blue flat-front shorts, brown sockless loafers, and a white buttoned-down shirt with the sleeves rolled to his elbows. He held a bouquet of flowers in his arms.

"You look fine," I told him, trying in vain to hide my jealousy. "You're never this nervous." I nodded at the purple tulips he held. "I'm sure Elle will love the flowers."

"They're not for Elle," Terrance said.

"Then who are they for?" I begged the question. I cursed myself for not doing the same thing.

"You'll see," Terrance replied, as we headed toward the house.

A double-wide, two-story, Victorian-style, Elle's parents' blush pink dwelling complemented the multicolor block of mint green, banana yellow, and strawberry red homes. The shotgun design featured houses as narrow as twelve feet wide, stretching deep into the back yard. The homes arranged rooms one behind the other with doors at each end of the house. Despite local legend saying someone could fire a shot from the front door to the back door without hitting anything, the design allowed for excellent airflow in the humid Gulf-shore summers before air conditioning became more commonplace.

Terrance opened the waist-high, metal gate on the fence that provided a boundary between the house and the public, red, brick sidewalk. I followed him up the five steps to the covered, bright, white front porch that was freshly painted. A few small, green shrubs added foliage to the postage stamp yard in front of the porch.

When Terrance rang the doorbell, he turned to me again. "You sure I look okay?" A dog barked inside the belly of the house.

Before I could answer, Sam and Elle met us at the door. "You gentlemen are right on time," Elle's dad jested with a broad smile. "My wife will be very happy."

A brown and black terrier twitched nervously around Sam's knees. The dog growled low at me exposing a few white incisors; a tuft of fur rose on the back of its neck. I took a half step back and held my breath.

Sam noticed my trepidation, bent down, and grabbed the dog's collar so it didn't jump at me. "I'm so sorry, Will. Beaux is usually friendly towards everyone. We even joke that he would lick a burglar. I don't know what's gotten into him."

"Bad doggie." Elle bent down inches from his furry face and scorned the suspicious pooch.

Sam held the door open with one hand and kept Beaux at bay with the other as I followed Terrance into the front room. I was thankful that Sam created obvious space between the dog and me. Music and conversation from multiple people in the back of the house carried to the living room where we stood. Elle eyed the flowers in Terrance's hands but waited patiently for him to present them to her.

"How've you been?" Terrance said softly to Elle as he slipped his free hand along the small of her back.

"Good," Elle whispered back with a smile she couldn't hide. "My dad likes you, so I'm sure my mama will too."

Not to further raise Beaux's suspicions of me, I silently glared at Terrance and Elle with narrowed eyes. What were they talking about? Were they saying what I thought they were saying?

Sam led us through the next doorway to the dining room. A long, rectangular, oak table with ten place settings took up most of the mint green room. A vase of white roses was centered on the big table.

A middle-aged woman with Elle's similar small stature met us in the dining room. She wore a light blue dress that accented her curves. She matched Elle's soft facial features but had brown eyes, unlike Elle's blue ones. Her skin tone was a shade lighter than Elle's, so I guessed Elle's Grandma Betsy was on her maternal side.

"Boys," Sam said, proudly enclosing his free arm around the woman's shoulders. He still clutched Beaux in his other hand. "This is my wife." He beamed at her as if he fell in love with her all over again.

"Please," she said, "call me Teresa."

Elle's mother turned to me and said, "Have we met? You seem familiar to me."

"I don't think so, ma'am," I told her. Teresa's brown eyes sparkled, but aside from giving Elle her good looks, I did not recognize her.

Terrance interrupted us and presented the purple tulips to Teresa. "Here, these are for you," he said.

"Oh, thank you," she said, taking them in her arms.

Teresa gushed over the flowers as Elle's initial desire for them turned to approval. Teresa carried the tulips and we all followed her to the kitchen. Nina, Nat, and Elle's three other siblings stopped talking amongst themselves at a small square breakfast table in front of the galley kitchen as we approached them. Teresa left us to put the flowers in a vase.

"Billie, Sarah, and Louie," Elle spoke to them, "I'd like you to meet Terrance and Will. I work with them at Antoine's."

"Good to meet you." Terrance extended his arm and shook each of their hands.

"So good to finally meet y'all," I said, as I gave a quick wave behind Terrance.

"You a germaphobe, Will?" Sarah jested. A small silver caduceus charm hung from a necklace around her neck.

"Yeah, somethin' like that," I replied, noticing her pendant. "You're the EMT, right?"

"Yes," Sarah chuckled. "I see my big sister has been talkin' about me."

"Only the good things," Elle interjected, nodding to Terrance and me. "I'll let them figure out the rest."

"Thanks." Sarah rolled her eyes. "I love you, too."

Sam finally released Beaux's collar as the dog relaxed on the hardwood floor at our feet. "Will you be good now?" he asked the pup.

Teresa returned with a vase full of the purple tulips and put them on the table near us.

"If y'all are ready to eat," she said, "let's go sit down. I've got crawfish pasta, zydeco green beans with Brabant potatoes, collard greens, red beans and rice, and burnt sugar cake for dessert."

"Sounds delicious. Thank you for havin' us. What can I help carry out to the table?" Terrance asked her.

"Oh, thank you," Teresa answered him with a smile. "Come with me and take what you can carry." They turned and headed for the kitchen.

"I'm helpin' too," I called after them, a few steps behind. Elle, Sam, and her siblings followed suit as we formed an assembly line behind Teresa grabbing hot dishes, water pitchers, and bread baskets.

Sam led the parade of dishes back to the dining room. He stopped at the head chair as we spilled out around him to the other place settings. Teresa took the seat next to Sam.

"Terrance," Sam nodded to the far side of the table. "Go ahead and take the seat at the end."

Terrance followed directions and sat at the end of the table. I sat to his left; Elle settled in at the other. Elle's

224

siblings filled in the rest of the place settings. Beaux rested on the floor beneath my feet, silently glaring at me.

"Before we eat," Sam spoke above his children to Terrance and me, "we thank the Lord for our blessin's." He clasped his hands together in front of him and lowered his head. Everyone at the table mirrored his gestures.

"We thank You, Lord," Sam spoke quietly, "for all you give; the food we eat, the lives we live; and to our loved ones far away, please send your blessin's, Lord we pray. And help us all to live our days with thankful hearts and lovin' ways. Amen."

"Amen," we all said in unison.

We passed serving dishes around the table. As each one came to me, I scooped a small portion onto my plate.

"You aren't hungry, Will?" Elle asked me, noticing the extra space on my plate.

"Ummm, I..." I stuttered, a little embarrassed that she caught me. "I had a big breakfast and I'm still full from it."

"It's okay," Elle said. "But don't skimp on the collard greens."

As Elle's family shared stories of their week, Terrance and I answered any questions presented to us. Beaux rose from the floor beneath me, rested his chin on the edge of my chair, exposing a few teeth and narrow eyes.

"Will you be my friend if I give you somethin'?" I whispered to him.

He let out a low growl in response.

I discreetly pulled some pasta and potatoes from my plate and held them low for Beaux. He sniffed the food, glared at me again, and then snatched the food up in one gulp. He settled at my feet again, lowering his head in his front paws.

For the next hour, the ten of us talked about our jobs, music, and the Saints football schedule.

"Daddy," Elle spoke up, "Terrance's mama is originally from Metairie."

"Is that right?" Sam acknowledged Terrance at the end of the table. "So is mine."

"Yes, sir," Terrance replied. "But now my parents live in Baton Rouge."

This caught my attention as I aimlessly pushed forkfuls of food around my plate. How did Elle know about Terrance's mother? Not too many people knew that information. Were Elle and Terrance spending a lot of time together outside of work? What about her not dating a coworker rule? What was happening in front of me? Terrance was not supposed to end up with Elle, I was. She didn't know it yet, but she and I were meant to be together.

I finally figured out what Madame Delia meant when she said time was running out.

CHAPTER 30

My Darling,   22 April, 1864

It is difficult seeing other couples around Vieux Carré. I get sad because you are not here with me. I know you are on your way in six more weeks, but my heart aches for you every day. It is difficult to breathe without you. When you finally arrive, we will marry at once and I will spend the rest of my life with you.

Yours forever,
Frédéric

After we cleared the dinner dishes, the ten of us relaxed in the family room at the far end of the house. Beaux had warmed up to me after I snuck him a few more bites from my plate. All of us filled out a white sectional couch that faced a brick fireplace. Matching floor-to-ceiling shelving full of books, photos, and knickknacks flanked the fireplace. A black Steinway piano positioned itself in front of double French doors leading to the outside.

"We can wait to have dessert and coffee," Teresa told us. "Let's sit awhile and talk."

Elle exhaled deeply in the corner of the couch between Terrance and her mother. I sat on the other side of Teresa. Sam, Terrance, and Elle's siblings were deep in conversation around us.

"What's wrong, *ma chérie*?" Teresa said to Elle, wrapping an arm around her shoulder. "But like your Grannie Betsy always adds to it, 'Gimme some sugah.'"

Teresa's words caught my attention because I hadn't heard that phrase in a long time, but I brushed it off knowing that many French descendants around here still might say the words of adoration.

"I don't know, Mama." Elle sighed. "When Will and I bought that sign for Auntie Viola, I found an old photo in the shop of a man standin' in front of the Beauregard-Keyes House. For whatever reason, I can't get the guy out of my head. We've been all over the

228

Quarter tryin' to figure out who he is. Will and I went to the Hermann-Grima House a few days ago askin' about him, but it's a dead end."

"Why are you so set on knowin' who this gentleman is?" Teresa asked her.

"I don't know," Elle lamented. "It's like we are connected. I can't explain it."

I listened intently to Elle's conversation with her mother without interrupting.

"Is the photo as old as the one we have over there?" Teresa nodded toward a small black and white framed picture on a shelf on the opposite side of the room. A mother held a child in the photo, but sitting ten feet away, I couldn't see the details of either.

"Maybe," Elle said. She rose from the couch and stepped across the room toward the bookcase. Teresa got up and followed her.

Elle pulled the picture frame from the shelf to examine it closer. Teresa hovered next to her daughter.

"Will," Elle called to me. "Come look at this. It's as old as the photo I have."

I stood from the sofa and joined Elle and her mother. Terrance continued talking with Sam and Elle's siblings.

Teresa pointed to a young blonde mother holding a baby in her lap in the photo. "This is my Grannie Angelica and my Great-grannie--"

"Oh my god," I gasped. Sweat pooled on my forehead and I felt like I was going to black out. My body tensed in panic. The whole room spun around me. Nothing else came out of my mouth because I was at a loss for words. My eyes darted everywhere as I tried aimlessly to steady myself so I didn't collapse to the floor. I stumbled toward the piano, clenching my fingers in an ivory silk vintage tablecloth that laid atop it. Seeing a "C" embroidered in it, I gasped and released it.

I bolted from the room leaving everyone wondering what happened to me.

"Will, are you okay?" Teresa called after me.

I left the room without answering her.

Moments later, Terrance found me pacing on the front porch, raking my hands through my hair. I wanted to scream at the world.

"Dude," Terrance berated me, "what's the matter with you? You're ruinin' this for me." His dark eyes filled with anger.

"It's Camille," I told him, finally standing still, though my heart still raced.

"What do you mean it's Camille?" he asked.

"The woman... the mother in Teresa's photo..." I stuttered, grabbed blindly at the air attempting to steady myself. "It's Camille."

"But Teresa said it was her grandmother and great-grandmother," Terrance countered. "How's that possible?"

"I don't know," I replied. "I don't know. But it's her. I'd know that face--those eyes--anywhere." A cluster of spark plugs fired in my gut. My breathing became more rapid, then shallow, then rapid again. I wiped my forehead with a shaky hand. Again, I felt like I was going to black out. "It's definitely Camille."

Elle opened the front door and interrupted Terrance and me.

"Will, you okay?" she asked. "You look like you saw a ghost."

What would I tell her? I thought I knew what happened but now this changed everything. I couldn't even comprehend what I learned moments ago. If I told Elle now, she might ask me questions that I don't know the answers to.

"Yeah, I'm fine," I fibbed, purposely flashing her a fake smile. "I needed some air."

"He'll be okay," Terrance reassured Elle.

"Okay," Elle said. "I can get you some water."

I nodded to Terrance. He understood my unspoken expression and escorted Elle inside.

After a few minutes of regaining my composure with a few long breaths, I entered the house and rejoined Terrance, Elle, and her family.

"Will, is everythin' okay?" Teresa asked.

"Yes, ma'am," I said, fanning myself, hoping to conceal my thoughts. "I needed some air. I felt a little faint. This hot weather is for the birds."

"Do you need some water?" Sam asked me.

"No, sir," I replied. "I'm good now."

CHAPTER 31

My Darling,   9 May, 1864

    I could not sleep again tonight because I was thinking of you. I want nothing in the world but your precious love. You make me feel alive. Thank you for all of your letters. I reread them often because you are always in my thoughts. This time without you has been unbearable. Enclosed is enough money for your passage. When you finally get here, I never want to be without you again. It would kill me.

Yours forever,
Frédéric

The next morning, I clenched my fists standing at the entrance of Madame Delia's Spirits shop. The initial shock of seeing Camille in the portrait had worn off. Now I demanded answers. Madame Delia was the only one who could provide them to me.

I entered the shop and pushed past the beads and gris-gris hanging from the ceiling. No one else was in the store this early in the morning. Madame Delia leaned on her cane behind the display case. Her wry smile left me unsettled.

"What happened to Camille?" I barked at her.

"Hello again, Will," she softly spoke.

"What happened to Camille?" I repeated, pounding my fist on the glass countertop between us. "I saw a photo of her."

"I told you before," Madame Delia replied, "what you think is not what happened."

"Tell me," I pressed through clenched teeth.

"Did you find the girl in the picture?" she asked.

"What?" I scoffed, annoyed that Madame Delia avoided answering me. "Yes. I don't care about the girl in the photo. I only care about Camille."

234

"I know you cannot pay me money for my information," she explained, again dodging my statement.

"Yeah, so?" I sneered. Anger boiled inside me. I wanted to knock the wooden trinkets on the counter to the floor.

"Finding the girl was your payment to me," Madame Delia said. Her calmness made me even more enraged.

"What happened to Camille?" I demanded again.

"Not what you think," she replied.

"Forget it!" I hissed, turning to storm off. "I died that day and I don't need you. Nothing you say can change that." I stepped a few feet away from the old woman, heading toward the front door.

"You know I am your only hope," she called after me. "Stop acting like a child who wants his blanket."

"But..." I started to say facing the other way, loud enough for her to hear me.

"You will do as I say," she spoke in an imperious voice. "If you walk out of here, you will never learn the truth."

"Fine," I spoke, more to myself than to Madame Delia. She held my fate in her hands. "You win."

With my back to her, I closed my eyes and inhaled deeply for a few moments. She was right. She was my only hope if I wanted to learn the truth about Camille. I turned to face her and, in three steps, closed the gap between us.

"Tell me about the girl in the picture, Will," Madame Delia instructed.

"Okay," I replied, hiding my discontent, even though I knew she was right. I pulled the ragged photo out of my pocket and put it on the counter in front of me. "Her name is Maria Dinu."

"Yes, I know," Madame Delia said. "She was my aunt."

"Well if you knew she was your aunt..." I countered. The expression on Madame Delia's face told me to disregard that fact and continue my story.

"She worked for the Baillairgé family as an au pair here in New Orleans," I told her.

"Yes, she left my grandparents in Romania when she was twelve," the old woman said. "They wanted to give her a better life here."

"When she fell ill with yellow fever," I explained, "the Baillairgés brought her to the medical ward at the Holy Family Sisters' Convent."

"That's now Bourbon Orleans Hotel," Madame Delia stated.

"Yes, I met the nun who told me Maria died there," I said. "The family also lost a daughter Adélaïde around the same time. They were devastated."

"Oh no... how terrible." Out of character, Madame Delia wiped a tear from her eye. "Where... Where is Maria buried?"

236

I continued, "The Baillairgés buried both girls at St. Louis Cemetery No. 1 then moved to the countryside."

"That explains why my family never heard from her again," Madame Delia sighed. "The letters stopped coming and we never knew why."

"I'm sorry," I said.

"Now I know where she is buried," she replied. "My grandparents assumed the worst but never knew where to find her. Even though I have a lot of spiritual connections, I struggled to locate her." She exhaled deeply, causing the wrinkles in her aged face to crease.

Remembering what the cemetery widow told me, I said "Yes, but her tomb isn't engraved with 'Dinu'. Since the two girls were buried together, the family marked it as 'Maria and Adélaïde Baillairgé'. I can take you to the cemetery someday and show you where if you want."

"Thank you for finding all of this out for me, Will," Madame Delia said. "You have found peace for my family." She raised her hand to touch me in appreciation but stopped halfway.

"You're welcome," I replied, finally empathizing with the elderly fortune teller. "Now please tell me about Camille."

CHAPTER 32

My Darling,   20 May, 1864
This morning while I walked to work at the port with Monsieur DuBois, I heard a woman singing inside her home. Her voice reminded me of you and the way you used to sing to me. Your voice could calm me on my darkest days. I could fall asleep to your heavenly sound. I cannot wait to hear your lovely voice again. I've been wearing the pocket watch you gave me every day since I left you. I hope this letter

arrives before you depart on the boat to come to Vieux Carré. I will meet you at the port in mid—July. I love you and cannot wait to spend eternity with you.

Yours forever,
Frédéric

"Very well," Madame Delia spoke. "You have made your payment."

I smiled at her, full of hope.

"Tell me what you think you know about Camille," she instructed.

"I'm tired of your ambiguous statements," I sighed.

"Please do it, Will," she softly replied. "Or should I use your full name of Frédéric William Boucher?"

I drew in a sharp breath at Madame Delia. No one had used my full name since *The Times-Picayune* listed my obituary in 1864.

"How do you know so much about me?" I asked her.

"You've already learned that Madame Delia knows things," she said, her silver eyes flickering. "Tell me what you think you know."

I puffed out a long sigh, preparing to tell my tale that only a handful of people knew.

"I came here from Marignane, on the southern coast of France near Marseille. I was engaged to Camille, the most beautiful woman I had ever met. I promised her a better life and so I traveled to New Orleans to earn money so that I could send for her. We wrote letters every week. I bought us a house at the north end of Royal Street and filled it with everything she could ever want. We planned to marry as soon as she arrived here."

Madame Delia nodded at me.

"I worked at the port for a commission merchant by the name of Pierre DuBois," I continued. "He introduced me to many wonderful things around the Quarter and beyond. He and his wife took me in as a son. I couldn't ask for a better employer when I knew no one else in the city. I told him all about my future plans with Camille."

"And then what happened?" Madame Delia asked as if she already knew the answer.

"Camille wrote to me saying she planned to board the SS City of New Orleans," I said. "And..." I paused and frowned, remembering the fateful day that forever changed my life.

"And what, Will?" The old woman settled against her carved wooden cane.

"I was sitting in Monsieur DuBois's office a week later and... and... I'll never forget what happened," I

240

stammered. I choked back a tear. "He brought in *The Times-Picayune* newspaper and laid it in front of me. The bold headline said 'SS City of New Orleans Lost at Sea. 191 People Feared Dead.'" I turned away and couldn't focus on Madame Delia. Tears streamed down my face. Even though that day happened so many years ago, I remembered it as if it was yesterday. "Camille was dead. The love of my life. Gone forever. I would never see her lovely face or listen to her wonderful voice again."

"Then what did you do?" Madame Delia asked me quietly.

"I was devastated," I told her through tears, turning back around. "Monsieur DuBois consoled me, but I ran out of his office. I didn't know what to do or where to go. As far as I was concerned, my life was over. I wandered through the Quarter in an angered trance, finally stopping at Jean Laffite's Blacksmith Shop at the far end of Bourbon Street. When I asked the barkeep for some whisky, he first handed me a glass. I shook him off, pounded on the counter, and demanded the bottle. Soon, I left the bar and took the bottle with me."

"Tell me more, Will," Madame Delia spoke, placing a steady hand on the glass counter between us.

She already knew the answer, but I obliged.

"I stumbled down Bourbon Street, guzzling that bottle of whisky," I told her with a crackling voice. "I remember stopping at Tujague's and getting a bottle of bourbon there. I don't remember who I talked to that night. The only thing on my mind was that Camille was dead and my life was not worth living." I wiped more tears from my face recalling how I never felt so alone, so lost. "The last thing I remember was stumbling in front of Antoine's and falling onto the sidewalk."

"Then what happened?" the old woman asked me in more of a statement than a question.

"I died that night," I replied. "My heart was broken. I wanted to join Camille one way or another. Only death could ease my suffering." I breathed out heavily. "Though I never found her. I have stayed at Antoine's since that night, still hoping to one day see my Camille again. Then when I met Elle, everything about her convinced me that Camille was reincarnated into her. Her blue eyes, her voice, the way she sang, her charm. I wasn't sure how she and I would be together, but I had to have her. I hoped that you could help me figure it out. I would have done anything to be with her. To me, Elle was Camille."

"But then you saw a picture of Camille last night?" Madame Delia spoke. I was not sure how she knew what happened at Elle's parents' house, but I had learned not to ask.

"Yes," I said. "She was in a picture holding a child. How is that possible? She died on that ship."

"No," Madame Delia spoke.

242

"NO?" I bellowed; my voice echoed in the small shop. Wooden trinkets on the nearby shelves fell to the floor from the booming sound. "What do you mean *no*?"

"Lower your voice, Will," the white-haired fortune teller warned me. "Do you want to find out what happened to Camille or not?"

"Yes," I said, bowing my head in shame for yelling. "I'm sorry. Please tell me about Camille."

"Camille didn't get on the ship," Madame Delia explained. "Days before she was supposed to leave, she came down with a minor case of pneumonia and didn't think she would survive the long trip. She decided to stay in France until she was well enough to travel. She wrote you a letter with her change in plans, but it never reached you. She took the next ship a month later. When she finally arrived at the Port of New Orleans, you weren't there."

"I wasn't there because I was already dead," I lamented, blowing out a sigh. Losing Camille was a hell I couldn't go through again. My body was already deep in a grave in Lafayette Cemetery, but my being still felt buried alive all over again.

Madame Delia continued, "At first Camille was angry that you didn't meet her at the port, but she kept all of your letters and pieced everything together. She went to your house on Royal Street. When she got there, Pierre

DuBois was packing up, getting ready to sell it because, as you said, he was practically a father to you."

"Camille came to New Orleans and found the house on Royal Street I bought for us?" I blinked in disbelief.

"Yes," Madame Delia replied. "She found everything you purchased for her and that she sent to you. The portrait, the bronze inkwell, the purple chaise. Monsieur DuBois told Camille what happened to you and she was grief-stricken and collapsed in his arms. He saw how heartbroken she was, purchased the house for her to live in, and gave her a job with him in his office. She kept everything you bought for her."

"Then what happened to her?" I wanted to know, still processing everything. This stunning news floored me. "Why was she holding a baby in that photo?"

"A couple of years later, she met a man by the name of Nicholas Faucheux," the old soothsayer explained. "They married, he bought her a home on Dauphine Street, and they had five children. The youngest, Angelica, is Elle's great-grandmother. Nicholas took good care of Camille and their children and provided them with a prosperous life. Nicholas loved her."

Madame Delia paused, sensing the jealousy in me. Slowly, she held up a hand to finish. "But her heart, that always belonged to you, Frédéric."

My thoughts tumbled over themselves as I processed what Madame Delia described to me. Words left me. I thought I knew everything and was destined to a life of purgatory without my beloved Camille. In my eyes, Camille died when her ship went down. Then, I drank myself to death because I couldn't bear to live without her. I waited for her all of these years. No wonder she never came. Every wisp of air left my being. Unable to speak, I struggled to move, stunned by what I learned.

Madame Delia spoke again, taking notice of my disbelief, "What color were Camille's eyes?"

"Blue," I recalled. "Like the sky on the sunniest of days. I could get lost in them."

I pondered the memory.

"When did Camille actually die?" I wanted to know, arching a brow at the elderly medium. "How old was she? How did she die? Was she sick?"

"Camille was 87 when she passed in her sleep," Madame Delia replied. "She is buried in St. Louis Cemetery No. 1."

"You mean I could have gone past her tomb when I was there last week?" I bellowed. As if underwater, I pointed a slow and warbled finger at her. Shock and outrage filled me. All of these years we were in the same city yet never crossed paths. Never once did I see Camille in my walks around town or by the cemetery. After Camille supposedly died, I never returned to the house I bought us because it was too painful for me. The memories of us haunted me.

Madame Delia nodded.

My mouth fell open, stupefied.

"Then I'm going to her," I spoke rapidly. "I have to see her. I have to find her." I turned and rushed toward the door.

"No. You haven't found her so far and you won't." The old woman's voice stopped me. "Camille has already gone through the light. She has found her peace in the next realm."

I turned back and shook my head. "It doesn't matter. I want to find her grave. I have to see her."

"I don't know exactly where her grave is. That is everything I know about Camille," the old fortune teller said to me. "You'll have to find it on your own."

"I don't care. I will find her," I said. "Thank you. I appreciate everything you've told me."

I headed out the door but stopped halfway and faced Madame Delia again. "I have one more question."

"What is it?" she said, her silver eyes widening.

"When Elle and I went through Jackson Square that day, why did you call Elle Camille if you already knew what happened to Camille?" I inquired.

"I wasn't trying to get Elle's attention," Madame Delia replied. "I wanted yours."

CHAPTER 33

My Darling Camille,

I have learned the truth. My heart aches all over again for what happened to you and me. Our love is still strong and I promise I will find you and spend eternity with you no matter how long it takes.

Yours forever,
Frédéric William Boucher

After spending most of the night wandering the Quarter processing the new information I learned about

Camille, I found Elle the next morning with her back to me in the large dining room setting up tables for lunch.

"Elle," I called to her.

"What?" She turned around to face me. She stood upright, with her chest puffed out. An annoyed expression filled in her normally soft face. "You were bein' weird at my parents' house on Sunday. What's goin' on with you? You need to tell me. You've been actin' strange lately."

"Yes, I know," I cringed. "I'm sorry. I promise you I have a good reason." I raised my hand to touch her in remorse but stopped halfway realizing I couldn't.

"I'm listenin'." Elle rested her hands on her hips.

Even though I now knew she wasn't my beloved Camille, Elle's fortitude still charmed me. I couldn't help but grin.

"It's a long story," I told her. I was unsure how Elle would react when I told her the truth. She was a nonbeliever. I had to choose my words carefully so that she wouldn't laugh at me. Or worse, freak out and never speak to me again. I didn't want to lose her as a friend.

"I don't have all day," she said.

I glanced at the antique clock on the credenza along the far wall of the dining room. "The lunch crowd is comin' in soon," I told her. "How about we go for a walk between lunch and dinner and I'll explain everythin'?"

"I guess so." Elle glared at me as if she thought I was misleading her.

"I promise you it will all make sense," I assured her.

"Okay," Elle replied. "I'll find you after lunch. If not, you're dead."

A few minutes later, I found Terrance and Chef Miguel in the kitchen chatting at one of the waist-high stainless-steel tables. Chilled bowls of shrimp sat next to them waiting to be used for shrimp and grits.

"Hey, Will," Chef Miguel called to me with a wave of his hand. "Come join us."

"I have news," I said. "This is big. Really big." I wasn't sure how I would explain this to them. What would they think? I could barely wrap my head around the fact that my love hadn't perished on the boat. That Camille had a good life, a husband, children, grandchildren. And it all connected back to Elle.

"What's up?" Terrance piped up. "You can tell us anythin'. We already know everythin' about you. You won't scare us off."

I chuckled at his ghostly humor. "Well…. You don't know *everythin'*. I didn't know everythin'. You won't believe it. I'm still processin' it all myself."

Both Terrance and Chef Miguel stared at me with inquiring eyes. They both accepted that I was a ghost but treated me like I was one of them. Over the years, I had to be careful so that patrons didn't see a tray floating in midair or a door opening on its own. Terrance and Chef Miguel always had my back. I owed them.

"Well?" Chef Miguel said, drumming the counter in front of him with his fingers. "We're waitin'…"

I inhaled a deep breath.

"Camille didn't die on the ship," I finally blurted out.

"What?!" they exclaimed in unison. "No way."

"How do you know?" Terrance asked.

"Do you remember that fortune teller I told you about?" I stated. "The one who I said was the real deal? She knew my name and everythin'."

"Yeah," Terrance replied. "What about her?"

"And how I thought I knew Elle?" I added.

Terrance nodded.

"Long story short, I found the fortune teller again and she wanted information only I could give her."

Terrance and Chef Miguel stared blankly at me.

"From the other side," I clarified. "She had me search for her aunt who vanished and, in exchange, she told me about Camille."

I shook my head, still processing everything. "Then, when I saw the picture of Camille at Elle's parents' house, I went back to the old woman demandin' answers."

"And she told you that Camille didn't die on the ship?" Chef Miguel asked.

"Yes," I replied excitedly. "Camille ended up missin' the boat because she came down with pneumonia. Only I couldn't have known that." I paused. Sadness swept through me for the loss of Camille all over again.

"And by that time, you were already dead and lingerin' around Antoine's waitin' for her," Terrance deduced. "What happened to her?"

"She married some Frenchman named Nicholas Faucheux," I explained. "I hate him, and I never even met the guy. They had five kids and the youngest one is Elle's great-grandmother."

"No way!" they both gasped. Chef Miguel cupped a hand to his mouth.

"Yes way," I said. "I still can't believe it myself. That's why all this time I thought I knew Elle from somewhere else. And she sings like Camille. I can't get over the resemblance."

"You haven't told her yet?" Terrance asked.

"No," I replied. "You have any ideas? You know she won't believe me."

"That's true," Terrance said. "She's a skeptic. We were talkin' about that last night at my place..."

Chef Miguel and I glared at Terrance as if he left us hanging.

Terrance blushed in response.

"I guess Elle quit her no datin' coworkers rule," I said.

"Yeah, well..." Terrance blushed again. "You can't tell her I told you, though. She wants to keep things on the DL for now."

251

I grinned at Terrance. My two friends were starting a new relationship and, despite my initial objections and now that I know the truth, I couldn't be happier. "Anyway, how do I tell her?"

For the next ten minutes, the three of us came up with my best options.

CHAPTER 34

My Dearest Frédéric,   *20 June, 1864*

I hope this letter reaches you in time. I apologize for not writing promptly, but I have been ill with pneumonia. I did not get on the ship that left on the first day of June because I was too sick to travel. I am feeling well and will get on the next charter that leaves at the beginning of August. I cannot wait to see you. We have already been apart for too long, so I apologize that I am delaying our reunion. I will meet you at the Vieux Carre port in September. I love you with all of my heart and cannot wait to marry you.

Love always,
Camille

After the last lunch table left, I met Elle on the sidewalk outside of Antoine's. The sugary incense from Leah's Pralines shop across St. Louis Street floated gently over the narrow road barely wide enough for two cars to travel. Above the confectionary shop, an older gentleman rested against the second-story iron railing observing the passersby below.

"Come on," I told Elle. "Let's go for a walk."

She eyed me skeptically. "Where are you takin' me? Is somethin' weird goin' on?"

"No, I swear." I held a palm up to Elle as if swearing to God, hoping to reassure her.

We made a left away from the restaurant and took the first left onto Royal Street. Nervous to start the conversation with Elle, we walked for a block in silence weaving our way around oncoming foot traffic.

We crossed over Toulouse Street when Elle stopped and poked a finger toward me. "Okay, what's goin' on? You told me you would tell me why you were actin' weird at my parents' house. Now you're quiet as a church mouse. You need to tell me right now or I'm leavin'." She half-turned back the way we came.

Elle's patience had whittled down and she had every reason to be annoyed with me.

"Yes, you're right," I told her. "I'm sorry. I said I would tell you and I meant it. It's incredibly..."

"Don't even say complicated," Elle finished my sentence. "I've been single long enough to know that sayin' somethin' is complicated is a poor excuse for not tellin' the truth."

"Okay," I said, heeding her cue. "I'll tell you everythin'. Don't hate me."

She peered at me with expectant eyes. Those soulful eyes again. So much like Camille's. I could drown in them.

"I'm a ghost," I told her.

Elle blinked once, stared a moment at me, and then laughed out loud. Her laugh came from deep within her soul as if it was the funniest thing she had ever heard. She bent over in hysterics and held her hand to her stomach from the absurdity.

Without moving, I patiently waited for her to regain her composure.

255

Elle howled at my expense, tears streaming down her cheeks from laughing so hard.

"Oh, come on, Will," she finally spoke through snorting hiccups. "You can do better than that. Is this a joke? Am I bein' punked? You of all people know I don't believe in ghosts."

I stepped away from her, up the street. Twenty yards later, I stopped at the corner of Royal and St. Peter Streets, the cathedral a block over to my right.

"Wait up, Will." Elle caught up to me, wiping residual tears of unbridled laughter from her face. "I'm sorry for laughing so hard. But you have to admit that was pretty funny."

"I swear it's the truth. Maybe I can convince you," I told her, as we passed Pirate Alley and Orleans Street. Swaying her would be tougher than I thought. Even though some ghosts walked through walls, I didn't have that capability. I held onto my ace knowing I could frighten her. "Do you remember the first time we went to One Eyed Jacks with Terrance?"

"Yeah," she said. "The bartender eyed me up for drinkin' Maker's Mark."

"Exactly," I told her. "But she didn't even acknowledge me."

"The place was noisy and crowded," Elle countered. "She was busy tryin' to get everyone's drinks. She missed you."

"Because she couldn't see me. How about that guy you thought was cute at One Eyed Jacks?" I asked her. "Don't you think he would have noticed me standin' right near him and yellin' back to you?"

"As I said, it was noisy and full of people," Elle replied. "Or he was ignorin' the freak like every other normal person in this town when they encounter a weird guy on the corner." She was right; New Orleans was full of eccentric people that most passersby usually disregarded. One day, I witnessed a woman only wearing clothes from the waist down wandering around Jackson Square. Her torso was painted bright orange. Most people in the nearby crowd gave her a quick glance, then kept walking.

"Okay, good point." We approached St. Ann Street. Blue and yellow fleur de lis banners flapped in the wind on the second-story balconies above us.

"Have you ever seen me drink anythin'?" I asked Elle.

"You said so yourself you don't drink," she replied.

"Touché. Who do you think turned the light on in the wine cellar your first week at work?" I asked.

Elle stopped and rolled her eyes at me. "Oh, please. It was a faulty electrical wire. The buildin' is old. Everyone knows that."

Obviously, Elle needed a lot more proof.

We traveled up Royal Street, crossing Dumaine. On the edge of the sidewalk in front of The Cornstalk Hotel,

257

an older gentleman in a brown newsboy cap perched on the edge of a metal folding chair playing a trumpet. Where else but in the Quarter could someone serenade us like that? I could jump up and down in front of this man and yell in his face and he wouldn't notice. Would that prove to Elle that I was a ghost? Maybe. But she needed more than that.

At the next intersection, we turned right onto St. Philip Street. Multi-story pastel private residences abutted the sidewalk with a handful of restaurants scattered in between.

"Where are we goin'?" Elle asked. Her short legs put in double-time to keep up with me.

"You'll see," I told her. "I have somethin' to show you."

We walked the outer perimeter of Chateau Hotel which encompassed an entire street corner. On the Chartres Street side of the old hotel, a white and blue tiled mosaic placard on the side of the building read: When New Orleans was the Capital of the Spanish Province of Louisiana 1762-1803 This street bore the name Calle D Conde. The narrow street was empty because not many tourists ventured this far. Most of the popular restaurants and bars were several blocks behind us.

"How much farther are you takin' me, Will?" Elle asked, stopping to lean against one of the old black horse tethering posts still cemented along the block. "We only have so much free time before we need to be back at work."

"It's up on the next block," I told her. "Once we get there, I promise you it will all make sense."

"Okay...." Elle's voice trailed off as if she didn't believe me but was still placating me. She stood upright and hurried alongside me. Even though I couldn't get a direct line of her face, I could feel her eyes rolling.

At the next intersection, I led Elle diagonally across Ursulines Avenue, stepped a few yards further, and stopped.

"We're here," I said. "This is it."

On the other side of the solid, eight-foot wall next to us, the Old Ursuline Convent was considered the oldest building in the Mississippi River Valley. Sixteen French nuns founded the convent in 1726 and then eventually ran a hospital and opened up school rooms to educate young girls. In the late 20th century, the chapel, buildings, and gardens were converted into a museum and hosted special events.

"You brought me to the old convent?" Elle asked. "What's that have to do with anythin'?"

"Hold on a minute," I told her. A couple of cars passed in front of us on the narrow street. "You stand right here." I raised my hand in a stopping motion. Before Elle could protest, I crossed the tight road and faced her from the opposite sidewalk.

"Will, what are you doin'?" she yelled to me across the street. "This better be good."

"Stop bein' so cranky and trust me," I called back to her.

CHAPTER 35

My Dearest Frédéric, *25 September, 1864*

You are gone. You are gone, my beloved, you are gone. I am devastated. When Monsieur DuBois told me what happened to you, I could not eat or sleep for a week. He checked on me every day to make sure I didn't succumb to the same fate. You were correct, he is a good man. He told me when I feel up to it, I can work for him. I miss you so much. I know you won't get this letter, but I want to write to you because you are in my heart and soul. I will never love another man the way I love you.

Love always,

Camille

I took a few steps up the sidewalk and posed at the bottom of a curved staircase that led to the main entrance of a bright yellow Greek Revival former mansion. I leaned against the black iron rail.

Elle watched patiently across the empty street, sometimes glancing in another direction, as I shifted my body back and forth a few times making sure I got my positioning just right.

I finally stood still. "There," I told her. "What do I look like?"

"I don't know," Elle replied as if I was wasting her time. "You're standin' in front of the Beauregard-Keyes House..."

"Yes, exactly," I said. "Now say it again."

Elle repeated robotically, "You're standin' in front of the Beauregard-Keyes House."

I froze and waited with bated breath for her to connect the dots. But she didn't.

"Say it again," I urged her, without moving.

"You're standin' in front of the Beauregard-Keyes..." Elle stated a third time. She stopped mid-sentence as the information sunk in. Her mouth stretched into a gaping grin. "Oh, I get it, you are posin' like the man in my photo. Nice one."

"That man in the picture is me, Elle," I told her.

"Oh, come on," she balked. "That's impossible."

"I'm tellin' you the truth," I replied. "It's me. Imagine me with a mustache and full beard wearin' a dark suit and top hat." I ran a hand against my bare chin. I wore a white button-down shirt and black trousers, like all of the other wait staff at Antoine's. "The picture was taken when I first got here, but I shaved the beard and mustache off because, as you know, it is stinkin' hot in the summer in New Orleans."

Elle squinted her eyes and cocked her head at me. "Okay, I'll admit you're similar to the guy in the photo. But come on."

"It's me, Elle," I told her again. "I swear to you it is. I wouldn't lie to you. That's why every time we went to a new place tryin' to learn about the photo, I continually told you that you'd eventually learn the truth. And you kept sayin' how much the man was familiar to you. It's me, Elle. And the pocket watch was mine."

Across the quiet street, Elle studied me suspiciously, resting a hand on her hip. She opened her mouth as if to talk but closed it again. After a few silent moments, she finally spoke, "Let's say I humor you and admit that it could be you, and you say you're a ghost, how am I able to have a conversation with you?"

"Because everyone who works at Antoine's," I explained, "can automatically see me and talk to me. It starts on their first day. I can't explain it but that's what happens."

"But what about the restaurant patrons?" Elle shot back.

"Have you ever seen me interact with one?" I replied. "They can't see me or hear me. I have to be discreet around them, so they don't notice anythin' weird happenin' like floatin' water pitchers or napkins. That first week you started, I caught a fallin' vase before it crashed to the floor. The table right there didn't even notice."

Elle thought for a moment trying to best me. "What about Mr. Howard at the bookshop? He doesn't work at the restaurant. He spoke to you," Elle countered. She glared at me from across the street, literally and figuratively holding her ground.

"That's because I flickered the lights on and off," I replied. "I have to do that so regular people can see me and talk to me when I want them to."

"He said it was a brownout," Elle recalled. "Nice try."

I continued, "Do you remember the waiter on the street who nearly knocked you over?"

"Yeah."

"I was there," I said. "But he couldn't see me or hear me, so he thought you were alone."

"You told me you were in the coin shop," Elle replied.

"That's because I wasn't ready to tell you everythin' then," I told her. "I'm sorry I lied."

"What makes me think you aren't lyin' now?" Elle demanded. She stared me down.

"You're a tough one," I muttered under my breath, then spoke loud enough for Elle to hear. "What about that night when I met your dad for the first time? I flickered the lights on and off at The Spotted Cat. Don't you remember?"

"I remember," she said, eyeing me. "But what about when you met my mama? The lights didn't flicker then when you came in my parents' house."

"That's because she was associated with your dad," I explained. "And your siblings too. Your dad even said that Beaux never reacted like that to anyone before. Didn't you think that was strange for a usually well-behaved dog?"

Before Elle could answer, a man walked in front of Elle on the other side of the street from me. "Please come here so people don't think you're shoutin' to yourself. I swear I can prove it to you." I had been holding my ace since we left Antoine's.

265

Elle huffed and relented as she crossed Chartres Street in ten strides, closing the gap between us. She stood next to me.

"Well," she said and raised her palm in a sweeping motion. "Prove it to me."

"Touch me," I told her.

"No," she protested, raising a palm to me. "That's weird. I'm not gonna touch you."

"Stop bein' so stubborn and do it," I replied. "Try to hold my hand."

With a huff and an eye roll, Elle obliged and slowly slid her hand toward mine, locking her eyes on the movement. As her fingers cautiously approached mine, her hand passed through a pocket of air where my palm should have been. She quickly pulled her hand away and cupped it against her chest.

"What the hell?" she gasped, glaring at me with daggers for eyes. "*What* are you?"

"Now do you believe me?" I spoke softly, fearing scaring her away. "My name is Frédéric William Boucher. I came to New Orleans in 1863 from France. Marignane, France. Not the Marigny. I died in 1864 when I drank myself to death in front of Antoine's because I thought my beloved Camille perished in a shipwreck. I've been lingerin' at the restaurant waitin' for her ever since."

Elle eyed me suspiciously, wringing her hands together as if she burned her fingers when she attempted to touch me.

"But I recently learned that Camille didn't die in the accident," I told Elle. "And that she links back to you."

"What?" Elle shrieked. "How could she link back to *me*?"

"That's why I was actin' funny at your parents' house," I calmly explained. "That picture that your mama pulled from the bookshelf..."

"Yeah," Elle's voice cracked. "That's my great-grandmother and great-great-grandmother."

"Your great-great-grandmother is my beloved Camille," I said. "The vintage linen cloth on top of your mother's piano is the tablecloth I bought for Camille."

"It's been in my family for generations." Elle gave me a hard glare, folding her arms across her small body. For such a tiny girl, I liked that she was tough on me and a little cynical. She and Terrance would make a great couple. I couldn't ask for anyone better for my best friend.

Elle slowly uncrossed her arms, inching her fingers towards mine. Her eyes darted from her hand to my face and back again. She reached toward my palm and cautiously stretched her hand near mine. When she flicked her fingers into the space of air where she should have touched mine, she stopped. Instead of pulling her hand back again, she locked her eyes on mine.

267

"It's true," she finally spoke but was still in shock at learning the truth about me.

"Yes," I said.

"Does Terrance know?" she asked me, without blinking.

"Yes," I answered. "He knows everythin' about me."

"And Chef Miguel?" Elle finally pulled her hand back closer to her body.

"Yep, him too," I told her. "They are the chosen few."

"And now me too?" she asked. The soft features in her face hesitantly returned.

"Yes," I told her. "I'm trustin' you with my secret. You can't tell anyone. Not even your family."

"What about Georgia and Charles and everyone else at work?" Elle pondered, realizing I spent most of my time with the staff at Antoine's and never told her where I lived or much about my background. "He told me he's worked at Antoine's for over twenty years. Wouldn't he question why you've never aged?"

"I told him I have good genes." I winked at Elle. "Like him, everyone else all knows me as Will, like how you first met me," I explained. "I'm an employee like the rest of the staff."

"And *you* trashed the restaurant?" she asked.

"Yes." I cringed.

"But why?"

"Do you remember how I told you that I thought I knew you?" I asked her.

"Yes," Elle replied. "You said it was my eyes."

"Yes, your blue eyes," I confirmed. "But I couldn't place them. When you sang in the wine cellar, it all came rushin' back to me."

"What came rushin' back?"

"I thought you were Camille because you sounded exactly like her," I told her. "My Camille. And you had her blue eyes. I thought she was reincarnated into you. Somehow, her blue eyes traveled through four generations to you."

"Maybe my brown-eyed parents and grandparents carried the recessive blue gene?" Elle offered. "My brother Nat has blue eyes, too."

"True," I replied. "I wasn't sure how it would happen, but I knew you--er Camille--and I had to be together again. I was goin' crazy tryin' to figure out how to make it happen. I trashed the restaurant because I freaked out. I'm sorry."

"Then you learned Camille was my great-great-grandmother," Elle said in more of a statement than a question.

"Yes."

"Is that everythin'?" Elle eyed me, still unsure how to take in this new information. "Is there anythin' else you're hidin' from me?"

"There's one more thing," I replied. "Do you remember that house you liked on the far end of Royal Street? The one you pointed out on our way to The Spotted Cat to see your dad play?"

"Yeah," Elle said. "What about it?"

"It's been remodeled," I explained, "but that was *my* house. The one I bought for Camille and me to live in. I planted the oak tree in the backyard. It was a tiny saplin' back then."

Elle took a few steps away from me and raised a bent finger to her chin. "If I got this straight, I've been talkin' to a ghost all this time and didn't know it?"

"Yes," I told her.

"And no one else can see you or hear you unless they work at the restaurant or are associated with someone else who has spoken to you or you blink the lights and music on and off?" she pondered.

"Yes... I mean no," I corrected myself.

"What do you mean no?" Elle caught me.

"Do you remember the old fortune teller in Jackson Square who called you Camille?" I asked. "The one you blew off?"

"Yeah, she was a joke." Elle rolled her eyes.

"Actually, she wasn't," I told her. "She's for real. She's the only livin' person I've met who acknowledged me first without me sayin' or doin' anythin'. That had never happened before."

"You aren't serious..." Elle pondered. "I mean how do you know she is real?"

"The old woman told me about what happened to Camille," I said. "She said she called you Camille to get my attention, not yours."

"And you believe her?" Elle arched an eyebrow at me.

"Yes," I said. "She said that Camille is buried in St. Louis Cemetery No. 1."

"There's only one way to find out," Elle replied, taking a step closer to me. "Let's go. Right now."

CHAPTER 36

My Dearest Frédéric, 16 July, 1866
I still know you will not receive this letter, but I wanted to tell you something that has happened in my life. Next month, I am marrying a man named Nicholas Faucheux. He is a good man, Frédéric. I am lonely in New Orleans. I considered returning to France, but I decided to stay because you loved the city so much. Nicholas will take care of me and give me good

companionship. He says he loves me and will always honour me.

Love always,
Camille

"We can't," I said.

"Why not?" Elle shot back. "I can call the restaurant saying I'll be late."

"Let me rephrase," I said. "*You* can't. The archdiocese only lets people into the cemetery through organized tours or if you have a family member buried there."

"Duh," Elle countered. "You forget that Camille is my great-great-grandmother."

"Right," I replied. "I almost forgot."

"However, I doubt that they would let me in because I have no proof of lineage with me," Elle groaned. "I'm sure they won't let anyone in without proper documentation claimin' their dead relative is somewhere inside."

"You're right," I said. I noticed a few passersby on the opposite sidewalk gawking at Elle having a conversation with herself.

"If what you're sayin' about yourself is true," Elle deduced, "you can go right in and no one will notice you."

273

"No one except for the other ghosts," I muttered.

Elle barked a laugh at my dumb joke. "You're serious?"

"Yes," I said. "I talked to William Faulkner at the book shop, several ghosts at Bourbon Orleans Hotel, and an old widow at the cemetery. They all approached me first and no real people could see them." I paused, waiting for her to respond. "And, despite what you think, William Faulkner groped you."

Elle chuckled, then squinted her eyes at me. She waved her hand in a top to bottom sweeping motion in front of me. "You're tellin' the truth about all... this?"

"Do you want to touch me again?" I countered.

"Okay, you win," she said, pulling her arm back to her side. "I believe you. I believe you are a ghost. Meanwhile, anyone who might see me on the street right now thinks I'm some crazy girl talkin' to herself."

"That's not uncommon in this town," I replied. "They might think you're drunk."

Elle laughed again. I liked seeing her crack up. Her wide smile made me whole and happy. She was a great friend.

"Let's go over to the cemetery so that you can find Camille's tomb." Elle stood in front of the yellow Beauregard-Keyes House and hooked a thumb toward Ursulines Avenue.

"You know it's about a mile from here," I told her. "You up for it?"

We walked away from the restored mansion now turned into a museum.

"Absolutely, or we could go a few blocks and get a streetcar?" Elle's eyes narrowed together, forming a deep V in the crease above her nose. "Oh, right... you don't do streetcars. Why not? You never told me."

"Because," I explained, "I almost got hit by one and my boss, Pierre DuBois, pulled me out of the street just in time. I could've died."

Elle glared at me without stating the obvious.

Her mouth fell open as she connected the dots. "I didn't come to a dead-end at the Hermann-Grima House?"

"Yes and no," I told her. "I worked for him, but I didn't buy the pocket watch from him. Camille gave it to me."

We hurried five blocks heading northwest on Ursulines Avenue to the streetcar stop at North Rampart Street. Elle paid the $1.25 for herself to board and I nervously joined her at the back of the vintage rail car. New Orleans was the first city west of the Allegheny Mountains to implement passenger rail service and still maintained low prices.

Many decades had passed since the last time I was on a streetcar. Twitching my hands together, I remembered my greatest fear. The old rail car click-clacked along the wide thoroughfare passing Louis Armstrong Park and Congo Square.

Ten minutes later, we disembarked the streetcar at the Conti Street stop in front of Our Lady of Guadalupe Chapel. The church was built in 1826 purposely close to St. Louis Cemeteries No. 1 and No. 2 to serve as a burial sanctuary for the city's twenty-three epidemics of yellow fever. The rumored-to-be-haunted building was the oldest surviving church in New Orleans.

We took the sidewalk on the left side of the chapel, crossed Basin Street, and stopped in front of the old, thick, cracking cemetery wall. Hurricane Katrina couldn't even knock the wall down. A few small tour groups gathered in front of the narrow entrance to the cemetery waiting to be admitted.

"Are you goin' in?" Elle nodded toward the groups of tourists. "I can wait here until you come back."

"Yes, I did that the last time I was here," I told her.

"I'll call Chef Miguel and tell him I'm running late."

I glanced over the top of the cemetery wall, nervous and anxious about what I would find. I offered Elle a timid smile. "Thank you for comin' with me. I'm glad you're here."

"Me too." Elle's lovely pool-blue eyes twinkled in return and she waved her hands in a sweeping motion. "Now get goin'."

I left Elle and slipped through the cemetery entrance. Once inside, I headed left along the inside Catholic wall vault and took the first aisle between the crypts to my right. Like the last time I was here, I wasn't exactly sure what I was searching for. The hot sun above me cast prisms against the marble tombs in spectral rainbows. Sparse trees provided little relief from the heat for the tour groups nearby.

Standing among the tombstones, I read each inscription. Some tombs were in such disrepair that it was impossible to figure out who was buried inside. I hoped Camille's crypt marker was still legible.

I leaned closer to a tomb, studying the aging marker.

"You're back," said a woman's voice behind me.

Startled, I turned to see the kind widow from the last time I was here. Again, she held red roses in her arms against her black mourning dress.

"Um, yes," I stuttered, turning to face her.

"Are you looking for someone again?" she asked.

"Yes, I am," I told her. I focused past her, into the massive labyrinth of graves ahead of me. The task of finding Camille seemed daunting. "Maybe you can help me?"

"I will be happy to try," she said to me.

"I'm lookin' for a woman named Camille…" My mind stalled thinking of her married name. Obviously, her crypt would have her husband's last name, not her maiden name that I knew. "Camille... Camille Faucheux."

"Hmm," the widow pondered. "That name doesn't sound familiar to me. I don't know a Camille Faucheux. I'm sorry."

I lowered my head in disappointment. Searching the complex cemetery could take days.

"I do, however," the old woman said, "know a Nicholas Faucheux. I haven't seen him in a while though. A week now. Maybe they're related."

"Yes!" I exclaimed. "He was her husband." My gut churned at saying *husband* when it wasn't me.

"I can take you to the area of the cemetery where I saw him last," she said.

"Thank you," I told her. "That would be great."

I followed the widow deep into the maze of assorted mausoleums. The small, marble, house-like crypts resembled a city in itself. We made our way past the Glapion tomb, likely the final resting place of Marie Laveau. Red and white carnations were laid at the bottom of the crypt from someone making a wish to the late voodoo queen.

We turned left after the popular tomb, made a right, and then right again. We made a left at the Italian tomb that I remembered seeing on my last trip here.

Once we found our destination, I hoped the widow would bring me back out to the entrance again because I hadn't left any breadcrumbs in the three-dimensional maze.

The widow led me to the left of the large Italian crypt.

"Here." She pointed to the large French mausoleum. "This is it."

"Thank you," I gushed. "I wish I could repay you for your help. It would have taken me days to find this."

"You're welcome," the old woman replied. "I'll leave you be so you can be alone with her." The hospitable widow turned and disappeared.

In front of me, the French vault stretched four crypts wide by four levels high. A hard knot formed deep in my gut. Even though Camille was gone, I was afraid to see what remained of her. I hesitated to take a step closer to the large tomb. My nerves paralyzed me.

Taking in a deep tense breath, I inched closer to the mass crypt.

I read the first three placards and exhaled at each one. The weathered inscriptions listed each person's name and dates. The fourth one stopped me in my tracks: Camille Faucheux. Loving wife and mother. 1841-1928

I wanted to cry, though no tears came. I had cried for her so many years before. She was my everything. My life, my death. I traced my finger along her name, willing myself to feel her again. I cursed myself for our ill-fated

279

destiny. Pain flowed out of every part of me. Heaviness filled me like the same day I thought I lost her. Numbness returned, raking my being.

I knelt in front of her final resting place.

"She never forgot you," a man's voice said behind me.

"What?" I muttered, too far into my grief of her loss all over again to answer coherently. I slowly turned around to see who spoke to me.

"Even though Camille lost you and married me," Nicholas Faucheux explained, "she always loved you. Even after she made me a widower."

"What?" I repeated, still shocked at hearing his words.

Dressed in a dark mourning suit and matching vest, he stood a few feet from me. A black homburg hat covered the last remaining wisps of his white hair. Deep wrinkles lined his aged face and brown eyes. Teresa's eyes. Elle's mother.

In one hand, he held a curved wooden cane. In the other, a pipe dangled from his gloved fingers. He seemed like a nice, decent man, but I still wanted to hate him.

"Yes, Camille married me and I'm a lucky man to have had her as long as I did." The man knelt beside me. His dark brown eyes stared lovingly at Camille's grave. "But she never forgot you." Nicholas glanced at me. "You were her true love. The love of her life. She wore that diamond necklace that you bought for her until the day she died. I was jealous of you for years."

Nicholas half-smiled at me, stood up, and puffed on his pipe. The suit he wore was top of the line. This meant he had the means to provide nicely for Camille and their five children.

"I was always a distant second to you. She never stopped loving you," his voice cracking. "She insisted that our second son be named after you." Nicholas puffed on his pipe. "Frederick was her favorite." He chuckled as if he remembered an inside joke. "She called him Fritz. Anything he wanted, she gave to him." Nicholas paused and stared at me. "I worried every day about that child and, if something would happen to him, I'd lose Camille like she lost you." He shook his head.

I couldn't help but smile that Camille named her son after me. She still loved me and wanted a part of me in her life, even if I wasn't with her.

"If... If... she lived a long life with you," I stuttered, finally finding my voice, absorbing everything I was hearing. Somehow, I found the strength to stand. "Why... why did I never see her at Antoine's?" The question now plagued me. Surely, she and Nicholas would have eaten at Antoine's at some point over the years. They had the means.

"Camille refused to go there," Nicholas explained. "She had learned you were lingering at the restaurant and couldn't bear to go in. She knew she might not be able to see you, but she didn't want to sense your heartache. The unbearable pain that she caused for you."

Tangled words caught in my throat. Without a sound, I gaped at him. My eyes were unmoving.

"I believe this is yours." Nicholas reached into the inside of his jacket. He pulled out a pocket watch and dangled it in front of me. My pocket watch. The one Camille gave to me before I left France. She must have found it with my belongings at the home on Royal Street that I bought for us. I forgot to take it with me the morning of my fateful day. "She carried it with her everywhere and wanted to be buried with it, but I couldn't let her. Not after everything I had given her and our children. I gave her everything in life, but couldn't in death. Not when she would be with you."

I stood motionless in front of him, processing everything he said.

"I loved her with all of my heart," he said, pocketing the watch. "Even though you were the love of her life, she was the love of mine."

I still couldn't find the words to speak.

"Adieu, Frédéric." Nicholas smiled at me and tipped his hat before fading into the sunlight.

"Adieu," I finally spoke, still stunned.

My being filled with a medley of emotions. Camille was gone and I had mourned her every day. But unbeknownst to me, our perfect love continued on while she lived. I was grateful that Nicholas told me everything about my beloved Camille. Peace enveloped me. Perhaps she and I would meet again. I didn't hate Nicholas anymore.

"Adieu, ma chérie." I traced my fingers along her engraved name a second time. "Until I see you again."

CHAPTER 37

My Dearest Frédéric, 27 April, 1870
When I learned the other day that a ghost haunts Antoine's because he is waiting for his long-lost love, I was first intrigued. But when I found out it was you, my heart shattered into a thousand pieces. It is my fault that you are there. I cannot bear to see you in that state. I will always love you, Frédéric, until the day I die.
Love always,
Camille

"Well?" Elle glared at me with expectant eyes as I approached her. She stood hands on hips along the outside of the cemetery wall. "I've been waitin' here for twenty minutes tryin' to guess what was happenin' in there. Did you find Camille's tomb?"

"Yes," I told her. An uncertain smile formed on my lips.

"And did you …." Elle waved her hand in a ripple motion as if she was finally accepting my supernatural phenomenon. "...see her?"

"No," I replied. "But I met your great-great-grandfather Nicholas."

"Really?" Elle's sky-blue eyes brightened. "What was he like?"

"A little dry and borin'," I said, immediately wanting to swallow my words that I slandered her ancestor. "I think he wanted a ghost duel."

To my surprise, Elle barked a laugh. "That's funny! No holdin' back, eh? Still fighting over a woman after all these years."

I couldn't help but chuckle. "He told me that Camille loved me until the day she died. Apparently, Camille insisted on namin' one of their sons after me. Your great-great-uncle Fritz."

"Oh yeah," Elle replied, glancing to the side as if she was recalling something. "I remember my mama

285

sayin' his name a few times. Said he was a bit unorthodox, but he meant well."

"Do you want to know what happened to the pocket watch from my old photo that you have?" I begged the question. "Camille gave it to me before I left France."

"What? Tell me," Elle wanted to know.

"Nicholas told me that Camille kept it with her and wanted to be buried with it," I explained.

"Well that's good, right?" Elle interrupted.

"No," I said. "He felt slighted that she loved me more than him and couldn't bring himself to bury the pocket watch with her. He kept it all this time."

"Kind of like a kick in the pants back to you," Elle muttered.

"Yup." I pouted.

"Well, even though you didn't see Camille, I'm glad you found the answers you've been waitin' so long to hear," Elle said. Her wide blue eyes filled me with joy. "I wish I could give you a big hug."

"Me too," I replied, with a slight grin. "But thanks for bein' here."

Elle and I left the cemetery and headed back to Antoine's.

Finally, peace filled me.

CHAPTER 38

Three and a half years later

Chef Miguel and I hung out in the bland, uncomfortable chairs of the hospital waiting room. He shifted his large body back and forth against the stationary wooden armrests that jabbed into his sides. A few other people settled in the row of seats behind us biding the time flipping through dog-eared magazines. Duplicate chairs lined the perimeter of the room. Paintings of serene beaches held the focus of each wall.

Above us, a TV blared the local noon news about the impending horde of tourists for Mardi Gras.

"I hate it and I love it." He nodded to the television. "I love that the restaurant is booked solid for two weeks but hate the extra mess on the front sidewalk that we have to clean up every mornin'."

"I hear ya, Chef," I concurred.

"The funny thing is," he chuckled, "is that if *you* went out and cleaned up the sidewalk, the drunk tourists wouldn't think much of discarded beads and streamers floatin' in mid-air."

"You're right about that," I smirked.

Three and a half years had passed since I told Elle my secret and she kept her word to keep it all this time. The rest of Antoine's staff still treated me like a real person, not knowing the privileged information. Even though I no longer waited for Camille to return, I still enjoyed working at the restaurant. My time to spend eternity with her would eventually come. I hadn't been called yet. Until then, I worked with my friends. Life--rather, death--was good.

"How long have we been sittin' here?" I asked Chef Miguel.

He rolled his sleeve up a few inches and revealed a watch. "An hour."

In that time, a young boy came in with his arm in a sling, an elderly woman in a wheelchair struggled to breathe, and a man half-dressed in motorcycle gear limped in.

We turned our heads to hear a small crowd of people bustling through the hospital waiting room door, stopping at the information desk. Elle's mom and dad rushed over to us.

"Did we make it in time? How's she doin'?" Teresa sputtered out.

Sam spoke before we could answer. "We're so glad you brought her. You rushed her right over from the restaurant. We're so thankful for that. Is she okay?"

"Last we heard, Elle was stable," Chef Miguel told them, nodding toward the secure hallway doors. "Terrance is in there with her."

"I hope my baby pulls through," Teresa prayed.

"She will," Sam assured her, taking her hand. "She's with Terrance. He'll take good care of her. Don't worry, my love."

Teresa and Sam settled in the empty chairs next to us. Teresa tapped her foot impatiently, too anxious to pick up a magazine from the adjacent square wooden table.

"She's gonna be fine." Sam placed a hand on his wife's thigh. "You know she will. She's strong."

"I wish I could be in there with her," Teresa expressed, her brown eyes full of a mixture of hope and anxiousness.

Another hour passed. Each time the secure hallway doors opened, we jumped from our seats. We hoped to hear news about Elle, only to be disappointed when another patient or a hospital staff member wandered through.

"Somebody tell a joke," I said, trying to lighten the restless mood.

The TV above us now displayed an early afternoon talk show highlighting how to dress on a first date. Teresa pulled a granola bar out of her purse and munched on it.

"Will," Chef Miguel whispered to me so that Sam and Teresa couldn't hear him. He nodded toward the double swinging doors that led to the restricted area. "You could sneak in there and check on her and no one would know."

"I already thought of that," I quietly told him. Elle's parents talked amongst themselves, oblivious of our conversation. "But you know Elle would be furious if she ever found out I did that."

"Yes, she would," Chef Miguel chuckled. "You'd be blackballed for months."

After another hour of watching other patients and staff go in and out of the secured doors, Terrance finally sauntered through. White, gauzy hospital scrubs covered his black restaurant waiter suit. Latex gloves protected his dark-skinned hands. He wore a matching gauzy net on his head and shoes.

"It's a girl!" Tears of joy streamed down his beaming face. "She's amazing!"

"How's Elle?" Teresa asked.

"She did great," Terrance answered. "She's resting now."

"See," Sam said, "I told you our baby girl would be fine."

290

We all jumped from our seats and congratulated him with hugs and kisses. I stuck to the outside of the group embrace.

A year ago, we all gathered for Elle and Terrance's wedding. I couldn't have been more proud to see my best friends get married. Elle was a beautiful bride. She was so happy and Terrance cried tears of joy. The ceremony was at St. Augustine's halfway between the Quarter and Bywater. And, of course, the reception was at Antoine's.

Earlier this morning, Elle's water unexpectedly broke in the middle of Antoine's kitchen. She wasn't due for another three weeks and her doctor allowed her to work as long as she felt good. She took it easy by only doing the lunch shifts. Terrance quickly called his in-laws about the impending baby as Chef Miguel and I assisted Elle to a hailed taxi.

Terrance and Elle opted not to find out the gender of the baby ahead of time and, much to our dismay, kept possible names a secret, like some of Chef Miguel's recipes.

"Tell us about her," Teresa begged.

"She's seven pounds, two ounces, and twenty inches long," Terrance gushed about his new daughter. "She's perfect."

"What are you callin' this little angel?" Sam inquired about his first-born grandchild.

Terrance met my eyes with his. "Camille."

The End

Thank you for reading my book.
If you enjoyed it, won't you please take a moment to leave me a
review at your favorite retailer?
One or two sentences are perfectly fine.
Thanks!

MARY WALSH WRITES

Sign up for my monthly newsletter on my website for book
news, recipes, and other fun things:
marywalshwrites.com

Connect with me on:

@marywalshwrites

Follow me on Goodreads:

www.goodreads.com/goodreadscommarywalshwrites

Made in the USA
Middletown, DE
24 September 2022

10723568R00175